America's Most
HAUNTED
CAMPUS

America's Most

HAUNTED
CAMPUS

William A. Kinnison

Library of Congress Control Number: 2018909622
ISBN: Hardcover   978-1-9845-4628-9
                 Softcover   978-1-9845-4627-2
                 eBook   978-1-9845-4634-0

Print information available on the last page.

Rev. date: 08/15/2018

To order additional copies of this book, contact:
Xlibris
1-888-795-4274
www.Xlibris.com
Orders@Xlibris.com
778785

For
Joshua, Hannah, Abigail, Alison, Emma,
Rachael, Paul, Sarah, Liam, and Noah.

It is not the ghost that arouses fear in you;
it is the fear in you that arouses the ghost.

CONTENTS

ACKNOWLEDGMENTS

THE HELP OF many people was involved in gathering these ghostly tales for the entertainment of those who have an interest in such things. First of all, I must express my gratitude to the many students, faculty, staff members, and alumni who have shared tales with me over the years. Especially I thank the many who, at their fiftieth class reunions, told long-held secrets. The more formal assistance of the staff of Wittenberg's Thomas Memorial Library was, as usual, phenomenal.

I express special thanks to Suzanne Smailes, Director of Technical Services, who also has oversight of the university archives. Equally noteworthy was the support of the staff at the Heritage Center of Clark County and its Fisher Family Library and Archives. I mention particularly Roger Sherrock, Executive Director; Virginia Weygandt, Director of Collections; Kasey Eichensehr, Senior Curator; and Natalie Fritz, Curator of Library and Archives.

For insight into the earliest years of the Mad River Valley area, I am indebted to my high school and college classmate, the late David R. Collins and his *Archaeology of Clark County,* Clark County Historical Society, Springfield, Ohio, 1959, 1979. I am indebted to David Raymond and Robert Morris for their more recent and more extensive analysis in *The Archaeology and Artifacts of Clark County, Ohio,* Clark County Historical Society and Ohio Historical Society, Springfield, Ohio, 2016. I express particular thanks to Kevin Laguno, Maureen Michaels, and Joel Cobb of Xlibris Corporation for their careful attention throughout the process of publication.

I am ever grateful for the helpful compositional, organizational, and editorial guidance of my son, William E. Kinnison. My wife Lenore has been very supportive of me in every way and of this project and tolerant of its intrusion into our lives.

INTRODUCTION

G HOST STORIES ARE not history; but the fact that they were very popular with students at Wittenberg and with Americans in general at the end of the nineteenth century and the beginning of the twentieth is history, and questions of why this was so are quite intriguing.

As president of Wittenberg, I occasionally told campus ghost stories that I had heard to groups of students on or about Halloween. The sessions taught me a lot about the playfulness of youthful minds and their capacity for imagining other than the usual possibilities. I did so in Myers Hall—known prior to 1915 as Wittenberg Hall or simply as Wittenberg—where most, but not all, of the stories seem to have originated. It was Wittenberg's first and, for thirty years, it's only building. The east wing was completed in 1848, and students moved to their abode in the forest across Buck Creek, north of town. Classes were still held at the Lutheran Church downtown. The center portion and west wing were finished in 1851, and all the school's functions then moved to the "wilderness."

I always ended our sessions by asking if anyone present had any strange and unexplainable experiences of their own to share. That usually sparked a flurry of tales of strange bumps in the night, rearranged furniture, and late-night footsteps that opened the possibility of yet untold stories for students yet to come. In these sessions, I related stories that I had found in student letters, student newspaper articles, old yearbooks, staff memoranda, and other archival materials or had heard directly from students, faculty, and staff members.

A student once described Wittenberg's ghostly tradition in the student newspaper the *Torch*:

> The next time that the darkness closes in, and the
> wind blows through the trees, rustling the crisp dry

leaves, and the owls come out, screeching into the clear and starry night, and soaring through the darkness to grab its prey from under the leaves, think twice about the spirited haunting that seems to frequent Wittenberg's stately campus. Do you believe the stories are true? For it is only if you want to believe that the truth exists.

I assured the students that these stories are only stories. It is not the ghost that arouses fear in you; it is the fear in you that arouses the ghost. Fear percolates through all your thinking, damages your personality, and makes you the ghost's landlord. These stories, however, I believe, do confer on Wittenberg a well-earned title as America's most haunted campus.

In writing a two-volume history of Wittenberg (*Wittenberg: An American College, 1842–1900* in 2008 and *Modern Wittenberg, 1900–2000* in 2011), I was struck by a number of ideas about the place's reason for being over its sundry decades and subsequent twists and turns of fortune. One was its focus in each succeeding era on a modern curriculum to prepare students for their future while grounding them in their nation's and the world's culture. Another was that the student was the school's primary reason for being. It was President Ort who put it succinctly: "Wittenberg had no quarrel with science" nor with useful education.

A third was that learning should be fun. As President Rees Edgar Tulloss expressed it: "If youth is the golden season for which the wise would barter all their wisdom, the rich all their wealth and call it a bargain, then it should be the joyous duty of those directing the studies of youth not to make education drab or dull or solemn, but to so enliven the process of learning that along with sound growth, youth may have joy in learning." Ghost stories were hardly suitable in a serious history, and the controlling ideas perhaps got lost in the detail of the historical narrative. Both, however, seem ever present in such stories as these, hence this third, thinner, and apocryphal volume.

The popularity of the modern American ghost story was very much a product of the nineteenth century. Science's challenges to religion created a climate of doubt, leading to experimentation in the occult with séances, Ouija boards, and similar games. Beginning in the 1840s, spiritualism was a growing national phenomenon. The carnage of the American Civil War (1860–1865) was traumatic for virtually every family, North and South, with the death of a million young Americans in a very short amount of time. The era also gave rise to the undertakers' and morticians' profession and created a new industry of funerary products, such as caskets, embalming fluids, and undertaker's tools. These industries became a major part of Springfield's postwar industrial growth. The century ended with the Gay Nineties and a new generation's effort to escape the dismal past. Ghost stories helped them do so. Later students saw them as sheer fun.

Do not be confused by my use of the first person singular voice in the telling of these tales. It is not that I was personally involved in any of them, but it is me telling the tale, repeating for you what others have told to me.

William A. Kinnison
Springfield, Ohio
June 30, 2018

CHAPTER 1

Unluckiest Room

Adapted from the *Wittenberg Weekly Wasp*, April 25, 1893

LATE IN THE night, many years ago, a student sat poring over his books in his room in Wittenberg Hall. Through the open screenless window came the sound of crickets shrilly chirping on the campus, the katydids scolding in the treetops, moths fluttering around his lamp, and an occasional beetle bumping along the ceiling. These were then common sounds now unfamiliar to us. He studied until he grew weary and then pushed back his chair and, stretching himself, began a great yawn. He stopped short suddenly and brought his chair down on all four legs with a thump. For there, sitting in an armchair at his side, quietly smoking a long-stemmed pipe, was one of the queerest-looking individuals he had ever seen. It was outrageous— no one smoked at Wittenberg, at least not openly. The rule was more lenient. Any student who used tobacco was expected to keep a spittoon in his room, and no smoking was permitted in any of the passages or around the building.

He must have come in through the open unscreened window because no one had come through the door. The visitor appeared as a short old man with a long white beard and wig, wearing a three-cornered hat, a frock coat, lederhosen, and low shoes with large silver buckles. He looked far too old to have been a former student, but so he presented himself.

"Well, I say!" the student finally exclaimed. "Who are you?"

Slowly removing his pipe as he blew out a cloud of smoke, delaying any possible response as pipe smokers always seemed to enjoy doing, the old man finally replied, "I am called the Flying Dutchman."

"The Flying Dutchman?" the student asked, puzzled. It was an odd name for any mother to give her son, I thought. Perhaps it was just a nickname.

"The very same," said he. "I came to this school in the eighteen forties and was expelled in about a month. To tell the truth," he said after another long puff on his pipe, "confidentially, I was a rather tough nut." Our conversation might have proceeded more easily, except for his infernal pipe.

Having thus introduced himself, he talked for some time, telling the student of jokes, pranks, and class fights of long ago. He continued smoking silently for a few moments more when he suddenly said, "Young man, do you know that this room of yours is a very unlucky one? Nobody who ever lived in this room in the history of the school ever came to any good. Have you not heard the legends concerning this place?"

The student looked incredulously at the little old man, quite startled and fearful of what was to come, but he said nothing. So the Dutchman continued, "No? Then I must tell you.

"The first residents as far back as I can remember were two country boys. They had lived on neighboring farms and had been very close chums from childhood. But having become disillusioned with the arduous life of a farmer, they looked for something better. They vainly pleaded with their fathers who were plain, matter-of-fact farmers to send them to college where they might prepare for a higher, more gentrified life. Such a prospect seemed unreasonable to both their fathers. They forbade it as many fathers did in those early years. Ezra Keller, the founder of Wittenberg, himself had been forbidden by his father to enroll at Gettysburg College in Pennsylvania, so he ran away from home with only fifty cents in his pocket and headed for the college. Even Abraham Lincoln condemned his father for opposing his every effort to improve himself by study and gentrification. The two young men in our story decided to leave home too and pursue an education on their own. Each left with the words of his father ringing in his ears: 'You are no son of mine, and this is no longer your home!'

"These two young men," continued the Flying Dutchman, "came to Wittenberg College and occupied this very room. They were hardworking students, stood high in their class, and were respected by all. That very year, however, typhoid fever was prevalent in this part of the country, and soon one of the boys was taken down with it. His chum, as roommates called one another, nursed him through his illness with great care until he too was taken ill. They were both of robust build and had good constitutions, so their fight with the disease was long and strenuous. But finally, in one night, they both died.

"To the intense indignation of all their chums, their fathers refused to receive their bodies. They refused to bury their own estranged sons. So one pleasant afternoon, they were buried by Ezra Keller and their fellow students over there where the science building now stands. They were the victims of their own ambitions, some might say, but they remain lost and restless souls wandering around this beautiful campus because they cannot go home."

With hardly a pause, the Dutchman continued, "The next occupant," he began, filling his pipe and forestalling his story in a long pause while the student grew increasingly apprehensive, "was a lean, lank fellow, a man of brilliant intellect but very credulous. He was made the butt of all the practical jokes of the other students, tormented and tortured by all, and by their frivolity that interrupted his studies. At last, on account of a serious hazing he had been through, apparently at one of the fraternities off campus, he became subject to temporary fits of insanity, generally late at night. Students coming back late to the dormitory would be startled to hear his strange cries and see him as a wild-looking figure running through the campus. It became a matter of fear and superstition for many, but at first, no one suspected the cause—grave sleeping, sleeping on a grave over yonder, northwest of Wittenberg Hall.

"One night, the students were more alarmed than usual," continued the Flying Dutchman.

Suddenly, with an exclamation, the student the Dutchman was visiting jumped to his feet, for on the wall was a monstrous shadow. But as it turned out, it was only a moth that had landed on his lamp chimney, casting a huge shadow before it burned in a flash of fire, giving off a dank and musty smell.

"As I was saying," continued the wrinkled old visitor, "one night, the students were alarmed to hear shriek after shriek issuing from this very room. Rushing in, they found the occupant's bloody body crouching over in the corner of the room. He was dead, killed, it was said, in a fit of insanity. His spirit is said to haunt the campus to this day.

"The next occupant," began the Dutchman, but he got no further. All this time, the Dutchman had been puffing on his pipe and was now so enveloped in such a huge cloud of smoke that the student could hardly see him. The smoke began to have its effect, and the student felt nauseous. He got nervous, and his dizziness increased until it got to be little short of downright agony. Unable to stand it any longer, he rushed from the room just as the Dutchman was beginning again to speak. After some time, he returned, pale and weak. But the Dutchman had disappeared as strangely as he had come.

It was only much later that the room's occupant recalled a different end of the story. His memory returned, and he realized that at the time, he had been actually caught up in the wake of the Dutchman's departure in a great gust of wind that had whipped him out through the open window into the gentle spring night air. He had whirled around the great hall in its stark isolation in that dark woods and over the cemetery and its eerie silence. When he awoke in his own bed, stirring from a long slumber, he was dazed and felt empty.

But the memory of his time with the Flying Dutchman was vividly and indelibly impressed on his mind, and he quaked at the slightest noise and was determined not to spend another night in that room. He slept little his last night, wondering what other tales there were about his unlucky room and what fate now awaited him as the present occupant. He was also distraught about what tales the Flying Dutchman might tell about every other room in that benighted hall. For surely, every other room on every floor, he feared, had its own forbidding history. If he were a malignant specter, he could empty the hall and destroy the college.

The next day, the student kept his resolution and moved to other quarters. All the other students wondered why he had left so suddenly,

WILLIAM A. KINNISON

but he never told them, thinking they would not believe him unless the Flying Dutchman himself showed up one night in their room. And if the stories are to be believed, he indeed visited many in their rooms. The haunting of Wittenberg Hall and the woods around it was surely the work of this very troublesome spirit, the Flying Dutchman. It is said that he enjoyed telling each occupant every room's own dismal tale, not just those in Old Wittenberg but in every room of every hall subsequently built and all about the old campus circle.

They were now alerted. Their task was to persevere and put the Dutchman out of their minds. If that proved impossible, They just had to overcome him. Whether he was a former student remained an open question because the school's earliest records were somewhat deficient.

CHAPTER 2

Ghost Host of Wittenberg Hall

SHORTLY AFTER HE arrived at the college, some of the upperclassmen inquired of the newly arrived new tutor whether he had heard of the genial ghost that occasionally occupied the fourth floor of the east wing of Wittenberg Hall. He replied that he had not and, furthermore, that he held strong convictions that there were no such lost souls; that most of us, through faith, were saved by grace; and that a few were forever condemned. But surely there were no strays lost in between.

He recalled that he had also said as much to the carriage driver who had brought him from town over the only bridge across Buck Creek; out the college road; past the Female Seminary; past that beautiful, cascading waterfall where the Mill Run plummeted thirty feet over the limestone cliffs into Buck Creek, the most beautiful sight in the beautiful village; and then up the circular drive to Wittenberg Hall. The driver had also asked him if he knew that this whole school was haunted. The upperclassmen who met him courteously accepted his pronouncements but noted that many matters were not so easily disposed of. They thought he would feel differently once he had encountered the hall's gentlemanly and congenial ghost, the veritable ghost host of Wittenberg Hall, who was himself a very good lad who did not believe in ghosts either. That was until he became one.

They offered to show him the grave behind the hall. He had noticed it, he said, as his carriage ascended the hill from the left, with its modest homemade marker and its surrounding white picket fence just northwest of the Hall. It acknowledged "David Burger, Excelsior, 1838–1856."

"That young man," the upperclassmen asserted, "formerly our esteemed, handsome, and likable friend, is with us yet! And you shall meet him."

When they showed him Davey's grave, they pointed to yet another nearby, that of the school's founder and first president Prof. Ezra Keller, DD, who had died in 1848 at the very young age of thirty-seven. They had not known him and, to their knowledge, had not seen his ghost—at least not yet.

They finally achieved what had been their objective from the start—shocking him. "You do know, of course," they asked, "that this campus was formerly the Woodshade Cemetery?" He was totally surprised, for that he had not been told. "There is a pioneer's cemetery in town on Columbia Street, where the earliest settlers were buried, including several Revolutionary War veterans," they added. When it was full, promoters of town expansion on the north side of Buck Creek opened Woodshade on seventeen acres. When the chance arose to get the Lutherans to locate their proposed college here, the same promoters offered the cemetery lands as a very competitive inducement, beating out the nearby town of Xenia that also sought the school.

To gain a college for a town on the frontier was a great boost to local real-estate speculators. It brought a steady source of school teachers and a cultural dimension to a rude frontier town. The Lutheran negotiators took the bait and got a cemetery in the process. Unknowingly, they increased the possibility of "haunts" on their campus since many residents had already been buried at Woodshade. The college as a fund-raising venture continued for some years to sell grave lots at $5.00 apiece, and any number had been sold. Several students who died too far from home to be buried there found their eternal resting place on their college campus. "Davey" was one of those, and the tutor was told, he had the further distinction of being buried in a grave that he himself had dug.

David Burger arrived in 1851 from Columbiana County, Ohio, to enroll in the preparatory department, occupying a room—he didn't recall the number—in Wittenberg Hall. There were so few grammar schools in Frontier Ohio that every college had to teach preparatory courses if they hoped to have any students ready for college level work. In 1852, Davey was admitted to the regular college as a freshman along with fifteen other young men. Had he lived, he would have graduated in 1856 and entered the seminary to prepare for the ministry. So forceful had been his personality that more than forty years after he died, his classmates still recalled him in their reminiscences. He was called Davey by his chums, a very likable young man with a face of strong features with keen black eyes, an overhanging square forehead, a prominent nose, and rather sunken cheeks. He was extremely thin, of average height, and with an appearance of hunger always about him. A serious young man he was, or so his classmates said, possessed of the liveliest sense of humor. He was the very personification of honor and manliness.

On October 24, 1851, just before Halloween, soon after he had moved into the college's whitewashed building, he wrote home the only letter in his own handwriting still in existence and now in the college archives. He began in the quaint style of that day, "After a long interval, I take up my pen to write to you." He got right to the point: "I remark that I am entirely out of money. I will give you the reason. My tuition was $9.33; room rent, $3.00; traveling expenses, $5.00; two week's boarding at $2.00; share of stove $2.25; mattress, $2.00; cot, $0.75; and books about $5.00." In addition, he had had to purchase firewood, a chair, a wash bowl, a lamp, and oil. He pleaded that he had been as frugal as was possible, but he had no pillow for his bed "till brother Yountz gave me one on condition that I will pay him when I got able."

"But with all my economy," he concluded, "I run ashore, and do not know how to get along as I cannot get work." On a positive note, he added, "But I deem it unnecessary to try to prove my economy as you will believe me." With a comment about how his economic plight affected his studies, he wrote, "And it is with much serious reflection that I feel it my duty to ask for aid." In conclusion, he indicated his determination "to fight my way through!" Such a letter, although it is not known if it brought results, surely qualified Davey for the admiration and respect of every out-of-pocket student of every generation. And it had been said that as time went by, Davey got acquainted with a great number of subsequent students as the redoubtable and oft reported genial ghost and host of Wittenberg Hall.

Within weeks of opening his school, Keller had gathered the more advanced students and organized a literary society, pouring into it all his zeal for debate, discussion, and rhetoric that defined a college education. Within months as enrollment increased, he divided the group into two societies to enhance the intellectual competition. Thus, there were two literary societies in which all the students participated and that dominated the students' out-of-class activities. They grew because of the students' love of current literature in that Romantic generation that blossomed on campuses long before modern lit was ever admitted to the curriculum.

The older society that David Burger had joined was named *Excelsior* after a poem by the young and still relatively unknown Henry Wadsworth Longfellow whom the members elected to honorary membership in their society. Longfellow acknowledged the honor and sent them a wall-sized poster of his best-selling poem "Excelsior" that decorated their hall for many years until it disappeared. A few members from time to time visited Longfellow at his home in New England where they were always well received. The second group was the *Philosophian Society* who had elected a young, flamboyant, and recently famed Edgar Allan Poe to honorary membership. He had just made it big with his poem "The Raven." Because of his dissolute lifestyle, however, he fell from favor and became an embarrassment. Faculty members encouraged them to forget him.

It may seem strange to later generations that poets were the "rock stars" of that romantic age of the 1840s. Parents and faculty warned their sons to avoid such characters, the very worst of whom were Lord Byron and Edgar Allan Poe who, as it turned out, were also the most popular among students. Poe had also written to the *Philosophians* a letter of gratitude for his election, since lost but accounted for in the index of his letters. He was much better known today throughout the world as a progenitor of modern literature, while Longfellow had sunk into obscurity.

The two societies locked in intense competition annually just as Longfellow and Poe did. Poe lambasted Longfellow as "lazy" and a writer of "shapeless" poems and a "literary pilferer" while praising his artistic skill and genius. He recognized Longfellow's capacity to demonstrate the ideal but criticized him for invariably ruining everything with his unrestrained compulsion to teach some moral in every piece he wrote. The aim of poetry, Poe said, was beauty, not truth. He won the hearts of students by insisting that a true poem was always no more than thirty minutes long when read aloud. To him, poetry was alive— an active experience—not a dull long chore.

Members of *Excelsior* were more focused on outward achievement and action and more pragmatic, ever upward and onward; the *Philosophians* were steadier, more reflective, and philosophical. The Excelsiors had a word for their lifestyle—"Excelsiorism" and each member was to be an "Excelsiorist." And they had a prophecy: "If it is right to conceive of a time when Wittenberg's faculty and authorities would forget the origins and destiny of the institution and let it fail, there are those gone out from the *Excelsior Society* who would gather at the grave of the sainted Dr. Keller and catching the echoes of the hymn which rose when its foundations were laid, would establish Wittenberg anew." Given the institution's uncertain future, the "prophecy" illustrates the youthful bravado of these western students.

In 1856, as a junior, Davey represented *Excelsior* as an essayist in the major annual competition in which orators, poets, essayists, and debaters collided. The annual contest was the biggest event of the college and equally popular in town as well. A student of talent and ambition prepared for the event with great gusto. For Dr. Sprecher, as for Dr. Keller, this was the seminal event in a student's education. It involved weeks, even months of hard work in which the student prepared to stand before his fellow students, the faculty, and a standing-room-only crowd in the town to do this one thing well. "One thing well executed," Sprrecher said, "is worth a whole lifetime of weak attempts." The many feeble acts do not make the man but one decisive academic struggle in his college years that has in it one's whole mind and heart determined to reach the high mark or fall in the noble effort. A student needed to only experience it once to be changed for life. For the student, it was Hamlet's "to be or not to be" moment or Martin Luther's dramatic "Here I stand, I cannot do otherwise" confession. It was what enabled them to change their world.

As the term ended, Davey became ill, declined rapidly, and died after an illness of just five days when most of the students had gone home for vacation. He was buried by those who lived too far away to go home in a grave he himself had dug. That situation arose when a classmate— one C. H. B. Davidson—died, and Davey dug his grave. Davidson's family, at the last minute, changed their minds and came to take his remains home. Davey was the next fever victim and thus inherited the open grave. The student body marched in solemn procession to bury him behind Wittenberg Hall on the ridge above the hollow behind Wittenberg Hall. For thirty days, all the students wore black armbands in his memory. The most curious and chilling thing for them that they could never forget was that Davey had dug his own grave.

The *Excelsiors* placed their small monument at the head of the grave and placed the white picket fence around it. For many years, they tended it well until all who had known him were gone. He was to lie there for eternity within view of the *Philosophian* Society's hall, reminding them of his great victory over them. As time passed, the fence became neglected, its paint peeled, and the slats disappeared one by one. The rumor was that students too lazy to hunt in the forest for firewood or too poor to buy coal had burned the slats in the stoves in their rooms along with much of the building's woodwork.

By 1874, the year women were first admitted to the college—two of the first ten were Professor Geiger's own daughters Alice and Lizzie— the monument to Davey had disappeared, and the grave had sunk below the surface level around it. Some said that the sinking proved that the occupant had abandoned his grave. Others conjectured that he just wanted to be nearer the fine young ladies who had enrolled but lived down the hill at Ferncliff Hall built where the boys' baseball field had been located and directly south of their bathhouse that also had to be moved. Others lived across Buck Creek in the town.

When the ladies enrolled, many of the men resented their intrusion, although they had looked forward to the change. They complained that they had to be better dressed, closer shaved, and better behaved; that they could no longer walk through the halls or go to class in their bathrobes and slippers. Those who saw Davey's ghost, however, always reported him as being attired in robe and slippers. From the day that Davey died, stories began to circulate about a restless soul in casual dress, wandering in the hollow behind the hall, along its ridges, and into the hall on its fourth floor late at night. Sometimes he was laughing, often confronting a student who was alone, talking to him in a strange language—actually he was reciting in Latin—or asking politely for something to eat. Yet as the years passed by, Davey dressed more stylishly and kept close watch on the ladies' hall.

The meeting rooms of the two societies were on the fourth floor of Wittenberg Hall, *Excelsior* at the east end and *Philosophian* to the west. Perhaps the frequent citing of Davey's ghost and the claims of hearing his laughter on that floor or in the stairway leading up to the east wing were accounted for by these facts. Davey's winning essay was in Latin too, of course, and bore a bilingual title "Quid Rides: Why Do You Laugh?" He had spent most of the year writing it and rehearsing its delivery aloud in the hallway, in the society rooms, in the cemetery, and in the surrounding forest, even in the cold shower by the college brook. His essay was an admirable piece of work, now lost, which even the *Philosophians,* the faculty, and townsfolk alike had lauded.

Davey, it was said, wandered through the hall in despair, looking for the assembly of his peers, reciting his essay in Latin that very few students now could understand. But he continued to ask, "Quid rides?" Was his essay a philosophical discussion of the American revolutionary credo of "life, liberty, and the pursuit of happiness?" Or was it happiness in the sense of sophomoric mischief? Or was his interest a more brooding psychological assessment of the fate of the "to be or not to be" student of his day, pondering the future? I think it probably contained something of all three.

Dr. Sprecher seemed much more interested in psychology than in any other branch of philosophy and spoke often of happiness in his

WILLIAM A. KINNISON

twenty-five years as president. "Happiness in this life is a reality and the attainment of it a practicable thing," he had said. "It is not a delusion." It was based on human views and feelings "of which we are as clearly conscious as we are of our own existence." It was not "a freak of fancy" but the result of rational reflection. "And what is education for," he asked, "if it did not lead to happiness?" All were sure that Davey had picked up Dr. Sprecher's practical, optimistic, and joyous view of the life of the mind, and Davey wondered why every student was not bursting with laughter over so pleasant a vocation as just being a student.

The hapless tutor as he closed his tale, reiterated that he was still not one who believed in ghosts, but was willing to go so far as to suggest that if per chance you should hear Davey in the dark night or meet up with him in his dressing gown and slippers in a darkened hallway or in the former Excelsior hall or out about the campus, you should have no fear. Davey, after all, is the happiest of apparitions, happy to be right where he is—atop the "hill of wise men"—for that is exactly what that old German word *Wittenberg* means. However, today we would insist that Wittenberg is composed of wise women and men. One duty Davey seems to have performed with great constancy had been to protect students who might be careless about firing the stoves in their rooms. How else had the building so miraculously escaped from burning down?

While it was widely believed that the ghosts of those who died or were murdered when they were young are particularly wretched and frightening, in Davey's case, that is simply not so. Offer him a pillow for his head or something to eat; cheer him on with his society's cheer "Excelsior Blue is always true. Philo White is never right." He will be kind to you, and he will tell you why you too should be laughing. Perhaps the two of you can laugh together because you are young and your life is all before you and you need only to find out what you want to do with it, what you were meant to be or not. There may be many who want to tell you what the answer is, but you will know. David Burger found out what he was meant to be—the friendly ghost and host of Wittenberg Hall.

CHAPTER 3

Ghost of an Unknown Soldier

THE FUNDAMENTAL GHOST at Wittenberg as described by students is a silent or grieving or menacing soldier looking for his lost army or his stray horse or just some enemy to fight.

He is less congenial than Davey Burger, more focused and determined than the Flying Dutchman. Some say it is the ghost of the notorious Gen. "Mad" Anthony Wayne, an extreme risk-taking and impetuous Revolutionary War officer sent after independence was won to the Ohio country by President George Washington. There, he became a merciless Indian fighter. In the process, he made the American Army a permanent force in peace and in war and set the nation on a course of Manifest Destiny. The first two permanent settlers in what later became Ohio's Clark County where Wittenberg was to be located had come to Ohio as suppliers to "Mad" Anthony Wayne's army.

Others say our ghost was a northern officer in the Civil War, hospitalized in Wittenberg Hall. I am sorry to have to tell you that that is a story of Gettysburg College—you know, the Battle of Gettysburg, the Lutheran seminary building there that figured so prominently in that fight. That building looks very similar to Wittenberg Hall because Keller studied there. He adapted that building plan to fit his Ohio site, making it somewhat larger in the process. All the stories about this ghost have one major flaw. Wittenberg Hall was never a Civil War hospital. A small pest house for students with contagious diseases was built in 1861, west of the campus entrance near the brook, but it hardly qualified as a hospital.

As the traditional story goes, the alleged Union Army officer returns periodically to the alleged place of his demise, late at night on the third or fourth or fifth floor—the stories vary—when all is quiet. He rolls a cannon ball the length of the hallway. It's rumbling sound and crash at the end of the hallway disturbs everyone in the building. It echoes and reechoes through the stairwells and from floor to floor until you are unsure of where the uproar originated. Tumbling from their beds and racing into the hallways, the building's sleepy occupants never discover the cause of their alarm. They find no cannon ball, no wounded officer, and no horse—only the startled and animated faces of their classmates.

"This session," student John Stuckenberg observed in 1856, "we have been troubled by students sent here by their father the Devil to disturb the peaceful rest of us all." He told of chairs pushed through walls, large stones rolled down the long hallways in the middle of the night, fireworks set off in buckets, and flaming paper balls raining down on passersby from open upstairs windows. He blamed it all on anonymous disorderly students, but could we really be sure? Perhaps he was closer to the root cause when he said that they were "children of the devil," a most alarming species of evil spirit. I do not believe in ghosts, but the Devil, we are told, commands a whole host of phantoms and demons all his own, the likes of which we should hope never to see.

Then there is the matter of the horse. Many versions tell of a ghostly horse returning to what must have been for it a very scary predicament. Presumably, the dying officer begged for one last reunion with that loyal and trusty creature. He persuaded his nurses to bring the horse to him on the fifth floor. Why any officer of so high a rank was hospitalized on the fifth floor of a building without an elevator seems implausible to the modern mind. Nor does the story take into account the difficulty of getting a horse up one flight of stairs, let alone to the fifth floor. In any event, after the officer died, they found they could not get the horse back down. Finally, someone shot the horse, and it was carried down. Even that was a formidable task. Ever after, students told of the ghostly officer on his ghostly horse riding back and forth in the hall.

Actually, there is a very famous legend of a horse in Wittenberg Hall, and although it has nothing to do with a sick army officer or the Civil War, it lends credence to the story. Pap Simons, the steward, had a horse. Simons was in charge of the college dining hall, and as often was the case with college stewards, he was not a popular man. He came and he went as a steward. He held pastorates in Maryland and Pennsylvania and, between calls, landed at Wittenberg where he finally settled. Students referred to him as "a broken-down preacher." He was called plain, practical, and of ardent piety. Religion, it was said, was the central and sole subject of his daily thought and the content of all his conversations. He had an overwhelming sense of divine majesty, the doom hanging over the guilty sinner, especially students, and the need to make haste to flee the wrath to come.

To that still Biblically literate generation, he sounded very much like John the Baptist must have sounded and looked very much like students would have expected the Baptist to look. Students believed Simons capable of living on locusts and honey and believed they could too. He thought students who still had time for the amendment of their lives more than anyone else needed to be warned of God's eminent wrath. He never failed to speak a word of reproof, admonition, or even, on a rare occasion, encouragement as he deemed appropriate as each student arrived to eat.

As students changed and Old Pap got older, he seemed increasingly out of touch. Though students always treated him with respect, they found his zeal an intrusion on the privacy of their meal times. In that less pictorial era, they carefully described him as a strong man with powerful jaws, large cheek bones, a big nose, quick eyes, shaggy brows, and a mass of dark hair that had a will of its own. He too once he had occupied a plot in the college cemetery had been said to make regular ghostly appearances in Wittenberg Hall at meal time. You will want to keep this picture of him in mind in case you run in to him looking for his horse.

Students conjectured that he had been a profane man but now used only one expletive of his own invention: "Byhold You!" When angry, he made striking gestures, shaking his whole body and, with a tossing of his head, shouting, "Byhold You!" Old Pap's horse was equally spirited. He rode him into town to get supplies. He pastured it on campus with the college's cows and kept it in the college barn. He took very good care of it. One student— Sam Ort— knew that each horse had a distinct personality, predefined and unpredictable to most of us. Sam seemed to understand horses. Simon's horse responded well to him, and the trust was reciprocal.

Late one night, a group of students, one of whom was Ort—later fourth president of the school—took the horse, muffled its hooves, and led him up to the fourth floor where he was found the next morning. When Pap learned of it, he was furious. He summoned Ort whom he believed was a horse whisperer who could talk to them. Ort stepped forward, boldly, helped Pap turn the horse around, and backed him down the stairs. As the chief culprit in the prank, Ort further ingratiated himself with the victim to the boisterous admiration of his chums.

Pap then mounted his horse on the ground floor. Amid raucous student cheers, he rode out through the front doors, saying his horse had now been through college and "Byhold You" that was more than "the worthless perpetrators of this deed" would ever accomplish. To this day, apparently, Old Pap Simons still busily searches for the perpetrators of this stunt, with a wrath all his very own.

There was a later story that Pres. Charles Heckert's horse had been taken into the hall's cupola in 1905. There was still another story to which I can give little credit, only because I know nothing that verifies it, but will tell you all the same. It has been rumored, though the facts were never publicly revealed, that a student was found dead in his bed in one of those "unlucky" rooms in the hall one morning, with the vague imprint of a horseshoe across his face that greatly disfigured him. The story does not seem to relate to any of the stories usually retold by students. Then there was a report from a lady who said her great-grandfather's brother rode his horse up the north stairs of Recitation Hall and into Hiller Chapel. For what purpose, no one has said. Nevertheless, according to student reports, Wittenberg Hall is surely home to one or more ghostly horses.

CHAPTER 4

Ghosts of an Ancient Valley

RETURNING TO THE matter of the military apparition in Wittenberg Hall, is it possible that this military ghost is not an American soldier at all?

If this suspicion is correct, there is no doubt that Wittenberg is indeed America's most haunted campus, just as there is no doubt that our ghost of Wittenberg Hall is not a Northern Civil War general, colonel, major, or captain. Nor is it "Mad" Anthony Wayne. No, Wittenberg's ghost is far more ancient than that.

There were early discoveries in the area near the college grounds that suggested that many of Wittenberg's ghosts may come from prehistoric times, from a society that existed here long before Europeans came to the new world. He was perhaps a descendant of the earliest occupants of North America who came after the ice age over fifteen thousand years ago. They traveled over a land bridge connecting this continent to Asia. There are modern archaeologists who suggest that there were pre–ice age humans in what we had the audacity to call "the new world" as early as one hundred thirty thousand years ago, but they may not have survived the ice age. There were at least three such migrations after the ice age, scholars claim, before the access route vanished. As the ice continued to melt, that land bridge was eventually covered by glacial water, and a great global warming began. By about 11,000 BCE it is believed some of those Asian wanderers had reached this very beautiful place we call the Mad River Valley. Even then, it must have been very attractive and became for them and later nomads a medicinal retreat and a dying place of great beauty for them. Eons later, it so attracted Ezra Keller that he persuaded his board of directors to plant Wittenberg Hall in its very midst.

The evidence of the existence of these ancient peoples and their burial mounds is state-wide, but Ohio seems to have been the most northeastern extension of the Mississippi Mound Builders' settlements. There are at least forty mounds here, 10 percent of all such mounds found thus far in Ohio. There is a great mound in Enon, a few miles southwest of campus, tall enough for a man to stand upright in its chamber. On the Bechtel family farm, west of Ferncliff Cemetery, near the bridge across Lagonda or Buck Creek, was another great mound. East of Limestone Street and south of High Street in downtown Springfield was an even larger one. There were many smaller mounds. East of town was an ancient fort, a place of refuge and defense whose earthen walls enclosed four acres of land. Half a mile north of that fort was a huge burial mound whose base covered an acre. The bones in this mound were said to be from a race of much larger stature than the white settlers who discovered them or the Native American tribes found here when European settlers arrived. The lives of the so-called Mound Builders in Ohio were more difficult than those of their brothers and sisters to the south as the uncovered artifacts clearly showed. The Midwest's colder winters and unpredictable frosts in spring and fall restricted the crops of maize and beans upon which they depended. It allowed for a more meager existence than they were used to.

Isaac Ward's farm, from which the city's Woodshade Cemetery and Wittenberg College were later carved, had at least three ancient mounds on it, twenty or thirty feet high and a thousand feet apart. The area for miles around the college grounds might well have been a prehistoric metropolis of ancient Indian settlements and graves and less formal interments. Their destruction may have a lot more to do with the restless spirits of Wittenberg Hall perhaps than we have previously thought. Altogether, the collection of forts and mounds indicate a settlement perhaps even larger than the later earthworks at Fort Ancient, forty miles further south, above Cincinnati.

The oldest cultures existed here in what is called the Archaic period, thirty thousand to five thousand years ago. The Glacial Kame culture left evidence of its rudimentary civilization by burying their dead in gravely hillsides left by retreating glaciers. Later they built mounds. Then from 700 BCE to about AD 600, there appeared what we call the Early, Middle, and Late Woodland periods. The Adena, Hopewell, and Fort Ancient peoples (using the names we have given them) characterized these periods.

These ancient peoples were the ancestors of the Native American tribes as the Shawnee tribe claimed. They left many indications of their presence: mounds, forts, earthworks, village sites, artifacts, tools, weapons – and graves. Evidence of all three of these Woodland cultures were unearthed in a single spot near the present-day Shouvlin Hall, near the ancient spring that fed the college brook and still flows below ground around the foundation of the Benham-Pence Student Center and into a modern storm sewer under Alumni Way. How all these varied relics of the three different ancient cultures came to be in the same spot is a mystery. Perhaps the spring was simply a place where white settlers dumped the product of a number of their explorations of relics of each successive culture. Or more likely, each of these groups, one after the other, had independently selected this same beautiful spot for a settlement.

Ohio claims more Indian mounds than any other state in the Union, and one of them was just down the hill a few hundred yards from Wittenberg Hall where there were too many students with too much time on their hands. It has subsequently been suggested that it was an Adena mound. It was near that centuries-old ever-flowing spring that fed the brook at the bottom of the hill. In addition to our ghostly soldier, some students report seeing in that area the apparition of a comely Indian maiden Winecheo walking along the edge of the brook, contemplating its holy, cool, pure, and continuous southwesterly flow.

The local newspaper reported on July 6, 1854, on a reckless student venture under the headline "An Indian Mound Opened."

> One day last week, a few enterprising spirits of the
> *Excelsior* society of Wittenberg College, undertook
> the excavation of a large Indian mound in the
> vicinity of the college. The task was toilsome. Others
> had attempted it before, but failing of immediate

success, had abandoned it. The mound was not of extra-ordinary size. Its height was near eight feet, and its diameter from thirty to thirty-five feet. After digging to a considerable depth, the students reached a stratum or layer of cement, resembling in its composition and order, our clay-burnt brick. After careful removal of all the ground from the surface, they could perceive in its outlines that it contained the bones of a son of the forest. They commenced a careful examination of the skeleton. The bones were still in a fine condition. The smaller ones, however, upon being exposed to the atmosphere crumbled to dust. In addition to the bones, they also discovered a very large whetstone—an abrasive stone used to sharpen tools and weapons—of the most beautiful finish and the finest texture, a number of very large and highly polished lance points, and various other stones, carved in the strangest possible style, and indented with primitive characters unintelligible to all. The young gentlemen have since been earnestly engaged in trying to decipher them.

Nothing in the experience of the students or their teachers enabled them to read their meaning.

This mode of burial is certainly unusually interesting. The body seemed to have been placed upon a beaten piece of ground, and over it this cement was then cast whilst in a liquid state. The body was placed east to west, aligned with the path of the sun's course, and not in a sitting position, as Indians generally bury their departed. The size of the mound, the care taken in positioning the body, and the relics found by its side, all indicate the resting place of a mighty warrior. Solemn thoughts filled each soul that stood around the tomb.

Pity for the wrongs and suffering of his race, moved every breast; and the truth conveyed by the following touching lines of [William Cullen] Bryant was felt by all:

> A noble race – but they are gone
> From their rich valleys broad and deep
> And we have built our homes upon
> Fields where their generations sleep.

These were solemn thoughts indeed. Once the challenge of the physical exertion and the excitement of the find wore off, the students pondered the age of the burial that did not seem to fit traditional notions of Biblical time. They pondered the meaning of their discovery and were haunted by its implications. President Sprecher told them of the value of science, geology, and archaeology for those who expected to be actively involved in studying the mysteries of the world. There were many such mysteries, he assured them, beyond their present knowledge.

Searching for truth, said Dr. Sprecher, would present them with a constant struggle and require their never-ending effort. It would challenge their faith. The life of the mind, he added, required constant, never-ending, and silent labor; it differed from physical labor but was labor all the same. "One should take neither an ancient declaration nor a modern one for truth without subjecting it to the closest scrutiny," he told them. "The educated person," he continued, "believed no creeds just because his father did. Nor did he accept the modern spirit or current novelty just because it enjoyed popular support. Both the ancient and the modern needed to be tested." Yet he advised them not to be of the common class who "picked up and devoured with avidity every new thing, every novel opinion, and every bold theory."

With the ending of the term and final examinations to be followed by vacation, the students were not as careful as they should have been in restoring the mound they had explored. They were careless about it, and as everybody knows, once a grave is disturbed, it cannot be restored to its original state. Some could not resist taking souvenirs. Our Stone Age

WILLIAM A. KINNISON

warrior, quite likely, was not at all happy about the rude intrusion into his grave. It was soon reported that he had found his way to the nearby Wittenberg Hall in search of his belongings and those who had taken them. According to student tales, it was he who returned periodically to disturb those who had disturbed him. In anger, he rolled a large stone down the hallway, and it bounced down the open stairway. They saw this ancient warrior only as their experience and knowledge allowed which accounts, perhaps, for so many conflicting stories about this particular apparition. He was perhaps not the only spirit from those ancient days to be among them.

You can only explain the roaming of these spirits on so many floors by the fact that it is a structure that is totally foreign to them in their life experiences. As for our warrior, he has no idea where the hall of the *Excelsior's* or their individual rooms were located. He gets lost because one room and its door looks like all the others to him, and he lumbers from one to another. Such a massive and many chambered pile is well beyond anything he could ever have experienced in his lifetime. But he knows that somewhere in that labyrinth, someone is hiding the very symbol of his authority—his large whetstone with its beautiful finish and fine texture.

On him, every worker and warrior depended to sharpen their tools or weapons. If you have the whetstone or it is hidden in your room, you had better return it to him as soon as you hear him coming. And by the way, he is not looking for a horse; he does not know what a horse is, for he has never seen one. After the ice age, there were none left in the Western Hemisphere until Spanish armies brought them in the sixteenth century. He is not a happy spirit such as David Burger nor an ambivalent one like the Dutchman. He is a very unhappy spirit and he is looking for anyone who might have ransacked his grave. Avoid him and others like him who are about, if you can.

It is quite possible, I am told, that somehow in our many intrusions, we have also aroused an ancient Native American prophet, a Stone Age ghost who is the very soul of all warriors, who seeks to rally these most ancient of tribes.

CHAPTER 5

Ancient Graves in the News

A VALUED CORRESPONDENT sends us the following interesting communication from the *Springfield Republic*, August 31, 1868:

> During the progress of the work at Ferncliff Cemetery, the workmen have frequently found traces of the remains of a human body lying not over a foot or two below the surface of the ground. These shallow graves show clearly the resting places of a race of aborigines, following the Mound Builders who also inhabited this region long before its occupation by the European man. The beauties of surrounding nature and the fitness of the soil at these grounds also led these people of the forest, like us, to choose it as a perfect burial place. Recently, while the workmen were engaged in removing some dirt at the work now in progress for a lodge and an entrance gate, one of the heathen graves was found lying close by the side of the ledge of the overhanging rocks with a flowing spring of water nearby cascading thirty feet to the river flats below.
>
> A few of the larger bones and a well-worn tooth remaining from decay gave evidence that the person had passed the prime of life when he died, and the frontal bone had the appearance of that of a man and bore evidence of having been buried for a great number of years. Nearby a decayed elk horn was also dug up. What was left of these mortal remains were carefully

collected by the superintendent of the cemetery and buried under a crosscut upon the rocks by the side of the entrance avenue, eighty yards below its former resting place, there to be secure from further molestation in the work of improvement.

The circumstances of this man's burial led the mind back to an unknown age and to people who inhabited this beautiful country of ours prior to its occupation by us. They lived and died without a written history. No monument or inscription was found over their graves to tell of their origin or their deeds. This heathen man whose body was laid in this romantic place by the side of this rock, no doubt spent his last days in wandering about the beautiful fields of nature existing here before they were changed by the art of civilized man. He was taught by the lessons of surrounding providence, and guided by the impulse of his depraved nature. He walked by the banks of the ever-flowing Lagonda, and saw in its waters the image of the Great Spirit and his maker.

The rich drapery of the great forest, the beauty and incense of flowers, the music of birds, and the wondrous orbs that shine in the far-off blue sky taught him to think of the great and wonderful Creator, and with no other revelation than this, he laid his body down to death, looking through the dim light of nature to a reunion in the spirit land.

How wonderful would it appear to this heathen man could he behold with his eyes the changes that have been made in the place of his former abode. To behold this busy city with all the conveniences and comforts of a civilized and Christian people; the railroad with its flying train, propelled by the power of boiling water; the telegraph with which we talk, as it were face to face with people beyond the setting sun; and the mysterious art of photography—with such things before him, his bewildered mind could not be made to believe that this was once his place of abode.

How mysterious are the dealings of Providence with his creatures. The generations of man follow each other like the waves upon the ocean, and the progressive spirit of man, like the rolling billows, either sinks or rises as these generations succeed each other. The lapse of a hundred years works a mighty change in the manners and conditions of the inhabitants of the earth.

The Discovery of Another Indian Skeleton at Ferncliff, *Republic,* August 25, 1869

Superintendent Dick of Ferncliff Cemetery and the men, with whom he is engaged in making the excavations for the house in progress of erection at the cemetery entrance, came up-on some interesting relics on Tuesday evening. Near a ledge of rock, and only about three feet from the surface of the ground, they unearthed a number of bones, evidently belonging to a human skeleton, the form, proportion and position of the parts being such to leave no doubt of their character. We have seen a section of the frontal bone of the skull, on which the positions of several features can be distinctly located. The place where the skeleton was found was so situated to lead to the inference that the body was not buried, but the person—whether man or woman cannot now be conjectured—lay down and died under the overhanging rock, which has since crumbled and fallen on the remains, the surface soil afterward accumulating in the course of a long series of years. The bones are in a state which to experienced eyes demonstrates that they must have been lying in the ground in a much longer time than has elapsed since any interments were made by white men in this region. They doubtless belong to some member of the aboriginal tribes which inhabited this valley, and if their story could be told it would very probably possess romantic interest to the minds of our modern race. This is the third skeleton that had been found within the limits of Ferncliff since the work of the Cemetery Association was begun.

CHAPTER 6

A Very Haunted Hall

"WE HAVE FOUND another ghost to raise Nichols' ire." So reported the *Springfield Daily Advertiser*, on March 5, 1872. Apparently, editor Clifton M. Nichols of the *Republic* did not believe in repeating ghost stories and was outspoken in his criticism of such reports.

> The other day as a clergy man of this city, who is not at all superstitious, was riding along in his buggy a few miles from town; he was startled by a voice, loud, clear and piercing, calling him to stop. He obeyed at once, looking all around to see who it was that wanted him. There was no house near and no person to be seen. He started again on his way, when he was startled by a series of the most heart rending shrieks which were full of human agony. He stopped again and attempted to find out what it all meant. The shrieks seemed to come out of the ground right by him. He could not fathom the mystery and drove on puzzled. There, take that, Nichols.

As Henry Wadsworth Longfellow, an honorary member of Wittenberg's *Excelsior Society*, expressed it:

> All houses in which men have lived and died
> Are haunted houses; through open doors
> The harmless phantoms on their errands glide
> With feet that make no sound upon the floors.

Wittenberg Hall was a blatant intrusion into this most beautiful primeval garden of the graves of Springfield's Woodshade Cemetery and those of ancient peoples who lived and died here long before we arrived. Amid our great joy at arriving at this beautiful place, most of us could not hear the shrieking from the ground upon which we walked. "This is a lovely spot," Keller said, "for the location of a literary institution." He also noted that Wittenberg's property included only a part of the great hill that dominated its surroundings and vowed to persuade the board of directors to purchase another seven acres from Isaac Ward to get the entire hill because that was precisely where Wittenberg Hall should be built. Perhaps there had been an Adena mound at the very top of the hill because the Mound Builders often selected such a dominant geographical site for their purposes.

The custom of housing young college men and, later, young women in dormitories for the purpose of educating them had been resolved in medieval Europe long before. It was undoubtedly an adaptation of the model of the monastic life since the earliest western schools had begun in the great churches and monasteries where accommodations were usually sparse and meager. But the politics by which each of a hundred generations of students worked out their interrelationships in such places was seldom discussed or written about in the histories. We find only random stories of pranks and bullying, class fights and tussles with "townies" in a hundred different college towns, and mysterious stories of lively student spirits who continued an education well beyond the standard academic curricula provided. It made for an entirely different situation from life in the family households from which the students came.

The struggle over rules to conform behavior began. The drinking bouts and belligerent games of the students of the thirteenth century were confused with pagan practices well into the fourteenth century. A code of behavior derived from church doctrine was to be the antidote. Trial by battle was still a cherished tradition for proving one's innocence or one's honor. Even the game of chess was prohibited because it led inevitably to gambling and life-threatening, honor-defending combat. Keeping fights out of the cathedrals and church buildings was difficult.

Tennis and football accompanied ale festivals and were soon outlawed in chapels and churches and university halls.

At Oxford and Cambridge, such pastimes were forbidden because they led to violence. The Bishop of Exeter railed against games played in his cathedral, which ruined the walls and broke stained-glass windows. Football was prohibited in London by royal decree along with quoits, throwing the hammer, handball, club ball, and golf. Similar rules were established at Westminster Palace. Only archery, apparently, was exempted because of its alleged contribution to national defense. Wrestling was the most popular sport of the day and generally outlawed at colleges and in college towns because it tended to induce riots. Knives often appeared in the most challenging matches. Consumption of alcohol at such events was common, and disputes among contestants and bettors led to further conflict. Rules multiplied.

The earliest dormitories in medieval Europe were cold and dark and regimented places. There were no stoves or fireplaces and no artificial lighting. Wittenberg Hall at least had a system of chimneys connected to each room where a student might attach a stove. Only if they were too lazy and improvident to lay in a supply of firewood or coal would they suffer very much. The intricate maze of pipes from every room to chimneys on the roof created a web of miniature tunnels connecting each to all, a channel for spirits some imagined, surely for rats if students were careless. The variation of firing skills and motivations among the students, however, provided for a constant fear of a fire that would burn the building to the ground.

Wittenberg Hall was a quarter of a mile from town. When a fire broke out—and it happened frequently—it took a runner some time to reach town, alert the volunteer fire companies, and get them organized on their way to campus. They dragged the fire engine over the bridge and out the college road, past the Presbyterian Female Seminary and the beautiful waterfall where Mill Run cascaded into Buck Creek, and up the steep road to the building. If students had not learned to respond with speed and great energy, the building would have burned to the ground while they awaited help. Their bucket brigades from the brook to the fire were lifesaving. Soon two great cisterns and a hundred leather buckets were just steps away from the hall's doors. Stoves were not the only menace. For light, students used candles or oil lamps, adding to the risks. As if the risk of fire were not enough, their lamps created a flickering of alternating bright light and near darkness, a perfect condition for ghosts and spirits to tease an occupant in a fearful mood.

Near darkness was always the great friend of ghosts. Most had no desire to be seen and had no mission to bother the student. Most were perfectly happy to come and go silently in the darkness. You might feel their presence while seeing nothing for certain. Telling ghost stories is always best in flickering and tentative lighting, such as by a campfire or in a shadowy candlelit room. Tales of haunting dwindled rapidly with the arrival of electric lights at Wittenberg in 1904 because ghosts whom you could seldom hear were also thereafter seldom seen.

In the romantic years of the 1840s, a man's home was said to be his castle and a personal reflection of his family's traditions. How could a combined "dormitory, classroom, dining hall, chapel" represent the personality of any one of its occupants or their families? It was more a unique beehive of activity than any kind of home, more and less than a hostelry to be sure but never a home. One of the school's primary functions was to get the boy out of his home and toughen him up for life on his own. Later a rationale to accommodate coeducation had to be constructed. The site, however, was a very defined environment of hallways, doorways, bedrooms, classrooms, a chapel, eating halls inside, cisterns and wells, the bathhouse, the pest house by the brook, individual woodpiles and coal bins, and the outhouse or *necessaire* outside.

Edgar Allan Poe, an honorary *Philosophian* at Wittenberg, saw such conditions as a conflation of two traditions—the Puritan and the Gothic. The first was essentially moral and religious and the latter psychological and secular, and they were inevitably in conflict. Between the two, the soul of the student was ground into maturity and adulthood. The building's fixed order and regulatory mood conflicted with each occupant's need to explore his own existence and to learn to manage his fears and compulsions. It was, said Poe, "as if we were all mad." A man's dormitory in these circumstances was often his prison, occasionally his refuge, and every so often his tomb. But it was hardly ever his castle.

A student in 1860 reported, "The space available for a dormitory was generally full from top to bottom, with at least two in a room. The college was a world in miniature. Here as in the real, busy world were ambitions, intrigues, envies, rivalries, tensions, and heart-burnings. Each man was to cope with his lot as best he could."

Students in such an environment in those early days had psychological needs but, until after Sigmund Freud, had no modern vocabulary to describe them. They fell into the biblical, sometimes pagan vocabulary of hauntings and temptations to describe their experiences. "Temptations at times crowd heavily upon me," said one occupant of Wittenberg Hall. "They assail me from all sides, from within and without." When he overcame one temptation, he lamented, another was ready to attack. He had reached the depths of despondency, he said.

"I am constrained to exclaim," said another. "Who is sufficient for these things? It is continual warfare." It is no wonder the college—all colleges, in fact—was visited periodically with unrest. The pent-up frustrations of students coupled with natural student exuberance set the stage for some kind of explosion, usually as winter ended. Some schools had religious revivals. Others had fights, serious hazing incidents, town-gown melees, and lots of property damage. More than one college president complained about rifle shots fired through dormitory doors. Disorder was more common than many would admit. Competitive games and sports returned as a way to let off steam.

President Sprecher noted that students were Jeffersonian, believing that their tree of liberty needed to be regularly nourished by the "bloodshed" of student rebellion. The students noted that Sprecher, however, could not discipline them without a tear trembling in his eye because he feared that he might catch an innocent amid the culprits. He let the harassed tutor-proctors who lived among the students carry that load. Sprecher always referred to college discipline as very much like "a well-regulated home." A century later, "Prexy" Stoughton talked about "the Wittenberg family," but a dormitory never really was a home, not a family but something else, something new to students as they grew toward adulthood.

On one particularly gloomy morning in 1866, Wittenberg's loyal student diarist, William Settlemyer, confessed that he was unwell, having passed a restless night in which his dreams disturbed him. He dreamed of "air loaded with an odor of fragrant flowers" and "the face of a lady unexpected and pleasant." Then he was at the home of one of his sisters in an unknown part of a strange city. Later he was with his other sister. He remembered that dream as a joyous experience, but later it seemed to trouble him. Most students did not write their dreams down, let alone try to explain them. Upon awakening, he said he spent the entire day in unpleasant labor and that he was ill-disposed to any study. He asked his roommate to have his sister send him a sugar cake. Later when it arrived, he described his fullness of joy and the anticipation of future pleasant associations and formal acquaintance with Julia "a model of sweetness untainted." Later on, a beautiful bouquet of flowers arrived at his eating club in town, addressed to the "Handsomest Man," whereupon he immediately claimed them as meant for him.

In a chapel talk in the 1840s, Ezra Keller sought to strengthen his students for contending with the world and its endless temptations. He outlined three "sins to which students are liable." First, he mentioned "the love of women." He was especially troubled, he said, by young men frittering away their important college years on courtship, going to parties, and running after and talking incessantly about girls. To this temptation, he added two others: pride and voluptuousness. Pride, he said, came from their privilege of a higher education to which less than 2 percent of youth in the nation at that time could aspire. Pride was an inappropriate response for such a great and unmatched opportunity. He urged them specifically not to be pedantic in speaking with the local citizenry. Voluptuousness, he implied, was the growing "dandyism" in dress of that Romantic age. Fancy dress, affecting a "Beau Brummell" display of sartorial finery in a frontier town seemed out of place to him. The tendency of the literary societies to outfit their halls with stylish furnishings—such as lavish chairs, carpets, and window dressings—was frivolous. If students concentrated on their studies, practiced religious piety, and attended to their duties in the literary societies, he assured them they would find that all their time and energy was fully and appropriately invested.

Adjusting to life in college and in a dormitory was the basic challenge for students. To that setting they brought and became responsible for their own personality and character, free to some extent to experiment and alter themselves. Fear and anxiety were the normal products of such a situation. Fear was, in fact, seemingly the fundamental emotion of mankind. It was the essence of the survival of the fittest, said some. It was first caused by the trauma of birth, said others, that universal experience at the very beginning of a life. From that moment forward, fear was to be our basic state of mind. It is that fear which the host of ghosts in Wittenberg Hall can sense and from which comes a given student's capacity to observe them.

The plan for a successful college experience was clear, simple, but not easy. Make every effort to master the courses of study required of you. Conform sufficiently to the regulations of the faculty so that the faculty will recommend you for a degree, which only they can do. Seek not to displease the board of directors too blatantly, and they will accept the faculty recommendation and vote to award you the bachelor's degree that the state of Ohio says only the board is empowered to do after they have assured themselves of your competence. It is not necessarily true that each party—board and faculty—will be influenced by the same conformities to which you might submit.

While you accomplish the above, however, and perhaps more importantly, you must also become sufficiently agreeable with your fellow classmates—the members of your own generation—so that with all your individuality, you are still acceptable to them. In the midst of all that, furthermore and most important of all, you must also be able to accept yourself as you are, for that, according to the philosophers, is the very definition of sanity. This is the real task at college; this is the path to adulthood. And it is not easy to accomplish.

CHAPTER 7

The Haunted Trunk

T HE TRUNK WAS owned by a graduate of 1881 who had entered in the fall of 1877 just as new house rules went into effect. We believe he entertained his chums by telling them how he had acquired it. It was advertised in the local newspaper as a haunted trunk, available at a very reasonable price to anyone who would accept the trunk with its resident ghost. The seller wanted its spirit to feel welcome by its new owner.

After graduation, the buyer traveled widely in the American West all the way to California, probably had a brief sojourn in Europe and pasted stickers on his trunk to show how widely he had traveled. He became an author and, later, a publisher and wrote a biography of the assassinated US president James A. Garfield who had died in the year he graduated. To our knowledge, he never wrote a word about the trunk and its resident ghost with whom he had traveled for so many years, but we hope one day to discover such a treatise. He was best remembered as a student for editing the school's first yearbook *The Aloha* in 1881 and for its tale of what we had always believed was an imaginary voyage with some fellow students and Professor Geiger in the good ship *Flying Dutchman*.

There was for many years a rumor of a number of trunks in the archives that on occasion created disturbances. An overworked archivist thought she heard rumblings from the trunks and made a strenuous effort to investigate them all. She did not find any ghost or other cause of the commotion. One theory was that long ago, an errant student had emptied his waste water pail out his room window in violation of rule 10. He then hid in his trunk to escape detection. He was trapped therein and expired while dorm mates thought he had gone away. They stored his trunk to await his return, and it was taken away when he did not reappear. Others believed he had irritated his roommate by seriously bridging rule number 17, being overly vexing, after which he inadvertently locked himself in his trunk. When he was determined to be absent, the trunk was moved to the basement where it was later discovered and put in storage.

We do not know exactly where this trunk of our 1881 graduate about which we first spoke now is. Since he ultimately returned to Springfield to live, it is possible that it returned with him and is somewhere about town in someone's attic or at the county's attic—the Heritage Center of Clark County that possesses a number of similar trunks.

Every college, of course, has rules. And those at Wittenberg in 1877, though more lenient than in the past, were still more restrictive than students wished. They were pasted inside the lid of this haunted trunk. The outside was covered with faded stickers denoting all the places it had gone with its owner and resident haunt.

Rules of Wittenberg College

1. The college bell will ring every morning at six o'clock, at which time every student is expected to rise.
2. At 6 1/2 o'clock, the bell will ring, when the students will assemble for worship.
3. At 7:00 o'clock., the breakfast bell will ring.
4. At quarter past 7, every student is expected to have his bed made and room swept.
5. At 9 o'clock, the bell will announce the commencement of study hours.
6. At 12 o'clock, the dinner bell will ring.
7. At quarter past 5 the supper bell.
8. At 7 P.M., the bell will ring for evening worship.
9. The recreation hours will be from breakfast until half past 8 A.M., from 12 until 2 P.M., and from 5 until 7 P.M., at all other hours, each student will be expected to be in his own

room so that all visiting must be done in recreation hours and AT NO OTHER TIME.

10. Every student shall keep in his room a bucket to receive the waste water and all rubbish that must be carried out of the house so that nothing of the kind be thrown out of the windows. Every one violating this rule will subject himself to a fine of 25 cents for every offense.

11. Every student using tobacco will be expected to keep a spittoon in his room, and no smoking will be permitted in any of the halls or passages or around the building, and **no chewing in any of the recitation rooms.**

12. Every student, during the winter session, must have his stove placed upon a sheet of zinc, and must remove the ashes from it at least once a week, and carry them out of the house in the iron buckets provided for that purpose.

13. No student shall play at hand or football or any game of amusement in the house.

14. No student shall play billiards, cards, dice, or any other unlawful games or at any game for a wager; or keep cards in his room.

15. No profane, obscene, or disrespectful language will be permitted. All violations of this rule, if detected, will meet with severe discipline.

16. No student shall play on any musical instrument or sing, or make any other noise, during study hours, or in any other way interfere with the comfort of his roommate, or other students in the building.

17. If any student shall be vexatious to his roommate, or shall damage and deface the room assigned to him, the faculty may deprive him of his room, or inflict such punishment as the circumstances of the case require.

18. No student occupying a room in college, shall board in his own room without express permission from the faculty.

CHAPTER 8

Woodshade Cemetery

TO ENTICE WITTENBERG to locate in Springfield, the town's promoters offered seventeen acres of land, north of town, across Buck Creek. It had been set aside by the town for a cemetery since their first one was rapidly filling up. The town had been disappointed in its previous failures to attract Antioch College or Denison University to locate in Springfield. To make certain of success this time, they agreed to offer these lavish acres and additional cash in an offer that could not fail. The Lutherans accepted the offer and, in doing so, not only found a home on the National Road but also a thriving cemetery which they continued to operate for a couple of decades.

The cemetery was not the only thing new students did not know about Wittenberg College. It was a distinction of sorts and something that would set the school apart from many, otherwise, very similar schools. Where else could you find such a distinctive "dimension" to your learning? As a student asked in the *Wittenberg Torch* in November 1991, "Do you believe in ghosts? If not, you are at the wrong school. Because in every nook and cranny, in every hallowed hall at Wittenberg, there linger spirits from eras long ago!"

When Ferncliff Cemetery was opened in 1863 in the middle of the American Civil War over slavery, the idea arose to move all the bodies from Wittenberg's cemetery to the new place. That was before Plum Street was cut through after 1869, separating Wittenberg from the new Ferncliff. The tale is told of one spirit that still wandered Plum Street, confused about where he should be—in Woodshade where he was first buried or in Ferncliff to which his casket was moved—apparently when he was out and about somewhere else. He might be the "old graveyard guard," frantically searching for his missing charges.

There was a widely held view in Europe that the first person buried in a new graveyard became the guard of all those who arrived after him. There are no records to indicate which Springfield resident was the first to be buried at Woodshade. The first student buried there was a local resident named Robert C. McCreight in 1847. Dr. Keller was buried there in 1848.

In any event, in 1863, all the burials on campus at Woodshade were to be moved to Ferncliff. Well, all but one were moved as far as we know. Some believe that perhaps up to ten bodies might have been carelessly left behind. But that's another story.

A short distance inside the Ferncliff gate, there is a large natural cave in the limestone cliffs along the road. It was of considerable interest to students who were delighted to explore every cave they could find in the school's neighborhood. City authorities developed this particularly large cave as a holding vault for those who died during the winter freeze when the ground was too frozen for the digging of graves. It was also used to hold bodies that were to be delayed for burial, needing further examining for coroner's inquests or for pending criminal charges. This cave was named Machpelah from the biblical story of Abraham's search for a place to bury his wife Sarah. Abraham chose the Cave of Machpelah. Ferncliff's Machpelah is not far from Plum Street and the campus.

One of the first to be buried on campus had been the sainted Ezra Keller himself. Keller's grave, according to Benjamin Prince, was not more than two hundred yards past the site of Wittenberg Hall that he had begun on the top of the hill. His body was later taken up and moved to a plot about three hundred feet west of the site of a later built Keller Hall now gone. When Ferncliff was opened west of the campus, his family had his casket moved once more to that beautiful place across Plum Street. He was buried then for the third time. By all traditional knowledge of such matters, I am informed, being so often disturbed was quite sufficient to arouse the anger of a man's spirit and cause him to haunt those responsible. It is also possible as we have noted that Ezra Keller could be the Plum Street ghost. We have little evidence of Ezra Keller's ghost elsewhere about the campus, except perhaps in one other place. But surely Dr. Keller, above all others, would not be a lost and troubled soul.

A student witness to the transfer of graves to Ferncliff was our diarist William H. Settlemyer from Pennsylvania. He wrote about all this body-moving in his diary on April 15, 1863.

> On yesterday I witnessed the removal of three bodies, two being interred 13 years and the other just six months. The former two were of course decayed, but one was partially petrified, in which might have been seen the form of that portion of the body, that exhibited sudden death from the corpulent appearance of the body. The other was blackened with foam exuding from the mouth, said to be the effect of medicine.

His was a straight forward, matter-of-fact recitation of a person who did not believe in ghosts, and it makes doubtful any sentiment on his part about disturbing other men's graves. But students lived closer to death in those days, and some of his fellow students were not as calm about it all. They worried about disturbing so many graves so near to the place where they slept at night and lived out their day.

It is rumored about campus that the early hazing practice of grave-sleeping in Woodshade Cemetery was shifted to Ferncliff at the same time the graves were moved, and I mention it as a warning. In "grave sleeping," a neophyte undergoing initiation is required to spend a night sleeping on a particular grave and reporting in the morning what he had heard, seen, and felt in the night. Some who have been required to participate in this activity have been said to experience wild fits of shaking and screaming.

There was one more surprise for the unsuspecting student—about the degree of "hauntedness" that might exist at Wittenberg. The Civil War greatly stimulated Springfield's growth as an industrial city. It stimulated the town's nascent prewar farm machinery manufacturing business so much that it would soon make the city the largest producer of such products in the world. It was, said some, the Silicon Valley of nineteenth century farm mechanization which led to an expansion of the world food supply.

A much more sinister-sounding business also developed in Springfield. There were massive numbers of deaths in the war, unlike anything before in the nation's experience. Few North or South homes were unaffected. A new profession emerged and a new industry began in Springfield to serve it. The new profession of "undertaker," or mortician, prepared bodies for transport across the country for burial at home. The war prompted a corresponding growth of casket and grave-vault manufacturing, the making of embalming fluids, and undertaker's tools, even the production of hearses. Springfield became a major centrally located industrial powerhouse in all these areas, euphemistically called the "funerary products" industry. In downtown Springfield, there is even now a historical library and museum called the Heritage Center with a tremendous, large, and intriguing exhibit of just such tools and products and a magnificent horse-drawn hearse. There is no better setting anywhere for staging the greatest Halloween vigil than that exhibit.

At about this time, it should be noted, Wittenberg's first recorded celebration of Halloween took place. The main gate of the Springfield Female Seminary grounds, the one designed to keep the girls in and the boys from Wittenberg out, disappeared. The next morning, it was found in Dr. Sprecher's classroom in Wittenberg Hall. The stairway banisters were covered with tar, and a steamer trunk from an unlocked room was dropped down the east stairwell from the fifth to the first floor.

To all intents and purposes, the information here related should, once and for all, end all tales of Woodshade Cemetery at Wittenberg, except, of course, for any graves that might have inadvertently been overlooked and left behind. That would mean, of course, that in some small or not-so-small way, Woodshade Cemetery is still here after all.

CHAPTER 9

A Ghost That Hunts

TODAY'S STUDENT IS unlikely to come into contact with the ghost I am introducing to you now. I must be careful in presenting him. I at first called him a ghost hunter, but that might lead you to think that he hunted ghosts. Actually, he is a ghost who hunts live game in forests which—thanks to the growth of modern civilization—no longer exist. As you can imagine, he has a number of reasons for being angry with us if, perchance, we come into his view. And while normally he will not see us, that does not mean that we will never get in his way. He is wily enough that he might still entrap you as you innocently go about the campus area. You should, therefore, be aware of the remote possibility of a fateful encounter, not with a ghost hunter, but with a ghost that hunts live game in his now long-lost happy hunting grounds.

In the early days of Wittenberg and well into the twentieth century, many students were happy hunters and fishermen. It was a time when the hunter was an emblem of independence and self-reliance, an icon of manhood, and the frontier spirit. Hunting and gathering in the west was a standard survival strategy for many a hungry student short of cash to buy food. The practice survived long after it was a necessity and even as late as the 1950s. That probably seems unbelievable to the modern mind. Springfield City Schools excused students, rifle in hand, from school for hunting season, and so did Wittenberg College. Many a fraternity boarding club served fresh game every November in their pre-Thanksgiving feasts in the groups that had a sufficient number of skilled hunters.

In the earliest of those olden times, at the time of the school's beginnings, one such student hunter wandered into the former lush

Indian hunting grounds stretching miles northwest of the campus. It was an extensive area much like the legendary Killdigan Woods west of Springfield, where wolf dens were scattered and, it was said, highway robbers hid out. It was at the foot of Indian mounds, early settlers noted, that wolves preferred to put their dens.

On one such excursion, a student came across an ancient hunter's horn. It was at this point that he made the mistake that brought him to the attention of the one who might not otherwise have seen him. Hastily wiping it off, he gave a single short blast to see if it still worked. As the sound wafted through the dark forest, with the pungent smell of its beautiful briar-free turf, he was startled as a ferocious Indian spirit, no doubt the horn's former owner, raced menacingly toward him. Was it perhaps a youthful Tecumseh, the most famous Shawnee chief to be born in our area?

The hapless student hunter's life perhaps passed before his eyes as he awaited a sure and instant death. What he should have known was that he was trespassing upon an area that was such an ancient hunting ground that the spirit of any native of the area going back thousands of years could be that angry warrior now closing in on him at such speed. For this area, just northwest of the great Indian medicinal garden that now comprised the Wittenberg campus and Ferncliff Cemetery, was the very center of the Shawnee Nation and center of native culture. In those earliest years, wild buffalo and great black bears and large elk were plentiful. As they arrived, hunters followed. The large hairy mammoth on display at the Ohio Historical Society Museum in Columbus, a huge specimen, had been unearthed in this county. In later years, smaller game predominated, and elderly and infirm natives arrived to spend their final days in this Garden of Eden. They met their more modest needs with small game, plenteous fowl, and streams full of fish amid the herbs and berries and nuts of their peaceful home.

As Europeans arrived, they invaded this ancient place and sustained life by poaching on the lands the Shawnee now used. On one occasion, a lone Indian hunter confronted a single European poacher, possibly Kentuckian Simon Kenton of local fame, in a life and death encounter like two elk, leaving only one battered but standing. It was something like the encounter our hapless student was having. There were many such random, isolated encounters in the area committed by lone assailants. One of the earliest white men born in the area hid as a lad in the cornfield as a small Indian party raided his family's farm, just carved out of the wilderness. He watched as all others in his family were killed, except him and his baby sister, and the cabin was burned. When he grew to manhood, he was known as one who, upon meeting up with an Indian, immediately shot him with no other cause than that early memory.

Chiefs of the area tribes and leaders of the settlers of Springfield and surrounding lands were anxious to resolve these random and isolated events to promote the greater security of all. In 1806, quite apart from the ongoing higher negotiations between the US Government and the tribes, they gathered in a peace conference of their own in Springfield at the southwest corner of Main and Spring Streets near one of the area's many ever-flowing springs. Their goal was to resolve matters closer to hand.

On this occasion, Tecumseh, the "Red Napoleon" as some called him, spoke on behalf of the Indians. He had refused to be disarmed and refused to smoke any pipe but his own. He told those gathered that he had been born just west of town and saw the area as his birthplace. According to legend, he was courting a young pioneer woman who lived south of town. He declared the innocence of the tribes of any responsibility for the random deaths in the area and assumed that the white men present were equally free of responsibility. "We, like you," he added, "have individuals among us who act on their own and for whose crimes the groups are not responsible." When Indians and settlers had resolved their grievances and peace was acknowledged among them, the Indians remained for three days, engaging in contests with Springfielders in marksmanship, with the bow and arrow, tomahawk, and rifle. There were contests of wrestling, running, and similar feats of individual strength. Within another twenty-six years, however, all the Shawnee were forcibly moved to a new home in Kansas.

The hunter rushing at our student poacher was said to appear whenever someone blew on his lost horn. At its sound, he came rushing to retrieve it. It is said to this day, however, that the student was not alone that day but was accompanied by a number of his chums. All of them fled as the ghost of the Native American approached, and the brave poacher delayed too long, seemingly frozen in his place. His timid, frightened friends watched from a safe distance, hoping for the best. They thought they heard the whistle of an arrow and watched their friend fall to the ground. The Indian retrieved his horn and left the scene as rapidly as he had come. When they approached their friend's body, the fallen student showed no sign of a wound where an arrow had entered his body. They were hard-pressed to offer any explanation for his death to officials at the school. Among themselves, they concluded that he had died of fright.

While the area over which the spirit of our hapless student poacher now roams is far more extensive than the campus itself, it is not unlikely that he is in this vicinity every now and then, perhaps looking for his erstwhile chums.

CHAPTER 10

Gregory

A PERSON KNOWN to us as campus grounds keeper and general all-around handyman Philip Gregory Smith, whom we call Gregory, was one of those people who, when you first meet them, seem to be someone you have met before. Gregory seems a timorous man and keeps his rabbit's foot for good luck with him at all times. Over the many years of his employment by the school, by various members of the faculty, and by the occasional student, he became well known for his cleverness in solving everyday problems. He was so efficient and helpful that no one questioned his authority for being there and doing whatever it was he was doing. Nor did they think to inquire very deeply into his background. He is referred to over so many years that it seems that he has been here all along, something of a ghost himself, perhaps with different names in different eras. His meticulous hard work and happy demeanor, together with an encyclopedic knowledge about various "haunts" as he called them, endeared him to all. He was an expert of sorts on that whole realm of things, yet he seemed deficient, as we shall see, in his specific knowledge of Native Americans, particularly the Shawnee who had inhabited this area before Wittenberg was founded.

"Do not talk so loud," Gregory warned students as he led them into an area of the grounds that was, he advised, "full of them." "You should not arouse them unnecessarily," he cautioned. Most haunts did not wander aimlessly about, he lectured, but always tended toward human habitations. "They gather around the 'higher quality people,'" he told them. "The better the quality of the person or the family," he assured them, "the more 'haunts' they had." He never ventured a guess as to why that might be so, if it were so. For instance, did the gentry have more secrets they feared might be revealed and hence dream of more ghosts around who might reveal them? Nevertheless, he was absolutely convinced of his theory. As one became more acquainted with him and more cognizant of campus ghosts, he seemed to be even more indispensable.

As preparation for a student's possible encounter with a ghost or apparition, Gregory advised that the most likely time for such an encounter was between midnight and three in the morning. Witches appear almost exclusively on nights with a full moon. A person born between midnight and one in the morning is more likely to see ghosts than others. A haunting is least likely to occur on Christmas because ghosts are barred from appearing on that day. Only Charles Dickens in *A Christmas Carol* has had the audacity to suggest otherwise, with a ghost of his partner Marley and three spirits who appeared to Mr. Scrooge between one o'clock in the morning and three in the morning. You can tell the presence of a ghost, Gregory always said, by the presence of ghostly noises and odd musty smells, the sweet smell of flowers, cold temperatures, a sudden drop in temperature, or by the sudden movement of objects with no visible cause. "Do not whistle in the night unless you want a ghost to confront you," he often warned. "Dogs can see them," he added with great assurance, "and they bark or growl when any apparition approaches." Horses too were nervous in their presence.

There were "good haunts" called ghosts and "bad" ones called poltergeists, he concluded, and you needed to determine as soon as possible which one it was that appeared to you. The Dutchman was probably a subdued poltergeist; David Burger, a ghost; and the ancient hunter, an energized poltergeist. As to why a ghosts is back among the living, he had a list of possible reasons: to avenge a wrongful death, to take care of unfinished business, to deliver information that had not been given before death, to punish an enemy, to protect loved ones, to give them advice, to reward them, perhaps to reenact his or her death, or perhaps for a reason the spirit does not understand.

There had been many stories of a gentle Shawnee maiden, Winecheo, a good ghost walking from the old spring where Shouvlin Hall now stands near Fountain Avenue. She strolled along the brook that flowed gently but constantly from the spring, under the rustic walking bridge and onto Buck or Lagonda Creek until new construction diverted its flow. It had been radically disrupted when the Phi Kappa Psi house, now the alumni center, and the Beta Theta Pi house, now old Woodlawn Hall, blocked it. No Indian would cross over water running southward, for such streams were considered sacred. Water from such sources, it was said, could cleanse an area of ghosts or any troublesome phantom. This gentle maiden, observed Gregory, was one of the campus's "good haunts."

In that same area, there was often the spirit of an older Shawnee woman at the spring, walking along the brook. He said he could not recall her name. Students should avoid her Gregory always said because there had been so much sadness in her life. Her brother as well as many of her friends had died in the wars. The spring in her day was in a weedy field and vine-tangled overgrowth almost hid the spring from view. Your feet might get caught in the soggy thicket before you knew you were there. Even at midday, it could be a dark and menacing place. There were the remains of a rotting old bench and an old chipped urn marking someone's resting place before 1840, before the cemetery or the college ever existed. The spot seemed isolated psychologically as well as physically. If you tarried there very long, you would very likely meet this old Shawnee woman. You would then experience, said Gregory, what it was like to "entertain an angry haunt who actually wishes you ill fortune." In some versions of the legend it was she who put a curse of rain on commencement morning, persuading Winecheo to agree.

The battle of the Shawnee Nation that centered on the Mad River Valley in 1780 was called the Battle of Pickewe and was the only battle of the American Revolution fought west of the Allegheny Mountains. It was just a few miles west of the area where the town of Springfield would be laid out in 1801. A twelve-year-old Tecumseh had watched the battle from a nearby tree. It was a fight between Gen. George Roger Clark, after whom Clark County would be named, and his one thousand Kentuckians against the Shawnee and their British allies. They had agreed to supply British troops with food grown in their area, and the British agreed to attack colonists settling in Kentucky.

Later in 1795, the new United States defeated the Shawnee in a final assault, resulting in the Treaty of Greenville that permanently removed the Shawnee from Mad River Valley. In 1832, when the town of Springfield was just decades old, all the Shawnee in Ohio were sent to the Kansas Territory. Wittenberg arrived in the frontier town in 1845.

In time, houses filled in the spaces around the campus as a little village—the college neighborhood—developed. With each new structure, the older Shawnee woman became increasingly unhappy. Samuel Sprecher, Isaac Sprecher, Michael Diehl, Hezekiah Reubush Geiger, Samuel Ort, Professor Young, and others acquired plots of land from the college—possibly in lieu of salary—and built large residences for their large families with large gardens and some chickens and geese. Each had its well. There were the college fields of vegetables, a grazing meadow for cattle and horses, a barn, and other buildings that organized a domestic life parallel to the place's major activity of education.

Ezra Keller had said that he felt quite like Martin Luther with all the unrelated domestic chores he had become responsible for. Students fresh from the farm were ripe with schemes to bring additional acres into cultivation, raising onions, carrots, and turnips to sell in the local market, aiding the college with the proceeds. They hoped it would underwrite more scholarships. Students, encouraged by faculty wives and, under the direction of Hezekiah Geiger, enlarged the cold shower at the brook to encourage cleanliness. Students called it congress because it was a great place for endless discussion with no pressing need to do anything about it.

Gregory was sure that it was all this domestic activity around the quiet spring and the babbling brook that made the old Indian woman so angry. The younger maiden was more puzzled than angry. There were others who also regretted the changes civilization was causing around the campus and the growing town. A young Benjamin Prince had described a "merry little brook" that began in a strong spring southwest of the primeval campus. It had flowed constantly for centuries, just like the beautiful waterfall where Mill Run Creek had cascaded majestically into Buck Creek until it became part of the town's enclosed sewer. A student had observed the waterfall before it disappeared and described it as a place of "leaping, sparkling, laughing waters." As the neighborhood around the campus developed, the constantly flowing spring and brook were finally diverted to flow around the foundation of the student center and into a storm sewer that flows under Alumni Way. The brook bed dried up entirely, except for an occasional and vengeful downpour of rain such as those that come quite often on Commencement mornings.

My suspicions about Gregory, I must confess, have never been satisfactorily resolved. He is such a useful man about the campus that I hesitate to pursue them too far. Gregory had read about the old Hindu Indian prophet Rakshasa who foresaw an Asian Indian paradise where those ancient peoples subjected in the British Empire would be led to a new life. Gregory quite mistakenly, in my opinion, insisted upon transferring that vision to his view of Wittenberg's situation. He asserted that Rakshasa would stir up a whirlwind in the ancient burial grounds in Southwest Ohio, providing a call to the spirits to a great dance that would gather them together and allow him to lead them toward a bridge to a great new land. He is said to hold in his right hand a rainbow and in his left a tremendous serpent, symbols of his power. He issued a warning to dissenting braves to not resist his authority and threw objects around and about them.

To divert our attention so we would not interfere, he created a great display of colorful lights in the midnight sky to preoccupy us so that he would be free to lead his people away to their great dance. Gregory justifies his use of this extraneous story by citing an entry in Ezra Keller's diary for the cold night of December 29, 1844 which verifies his action.

> Last night, after dark, I returned from a visit to the country. It was a beautiful starlit night. All was calm, and no sound was heard, save the low rippling murmur of the stream, which seemed to be the last note of nature's evening hymn. The sky was crowded with pure twinkling luminaries. They all smiled in their ethereal residency, their unearthly brilliancy. As I thought of their number, their magnitude, their

velocity, their undeviating obedience to their creator and perhaps their myriads of unfallen and perchance justified spirits, I was overwhelmed with a sense of my utter insignificance.

It is difficult indeed to tell our most gracious and helpful and clever Gregory—campus grounds keeper, all around handyman, and ghost advisor—that in this application, he is undoubtedly in error.

CHAPTER 11

Diehl House

APPARENTLY, IT IS not a question of whether Diehl House has its own resident ghost. The question is "Who is she?" One would think it would be an easy matter to find out. The house has had relatively few occupants. It is said that a ghost will not speak first but will always wait for you to speak. It seems, however, that none of those who claim to have seen this lovely apparition have had the presence of mind to greet her and introduce themselves. If they had, surely she would have responded by telling them who she was.

The house is one of the oldest in the campus area. The Samuel Sprecher House was next door to Wittenberg Hall, on the east campus drive. For a time, it served as the campus health center and was demolished for the building of Weaver Chapel. The Isaac Sprecher House built by Samuel's nephew was on the southeast corner of Wittenberg Avenue and Ward Street at the campus entrance. Diehl House is just south of Isaac Sprecher's house on Wittenberg Avenue. Professor Geiger's house was blocks away, facing Springfield across the cliffs. These were the houses of Wittenberg's founders. Ezra Keller died before the campus was developed and had lived in town on High Street, a block west of the Lutheran Church. That house has long since been torn down.

Michael Diehl, a professor of ancient languages, came from Gettysburg Seminary in 1846. He served as an acting president when Ezra Keller died in 1848 and was the author of Keller's biography which was a very popular book among faculty, students, and many residents in the town. A religious man, Diehl built his house in a cruciform shape with a front parlor and a sitting room behind it in Victorian style. It was a ten-room house with a graceful spiral staircase. He and his wife,

Harriet Winwood, daughter of the first college treasurer, raised several children there.

When Professor Diehl died, Mrs. Diehl was unable to keep the house. Ira Chorpening, the new college treasurer, occupied the house for about five years, after which it was sold to Robert Q. King, a local businessman. King's daughter later sold it to Lee and Beatrice "Bebe" Bayley in 1925. At the death of Mrs. Bayley in 1989, the house was given to Wittenberg and was used as a guest house.

But the question remains. Who is the charming lady ghost of Diehl House? Is it Harriet Diehl or a daughter? Perhaps it is the lovely Mrs. Chorpening or one of her daughters. Perhaps it is an even later occupant. After all, Mrs. "Bebe" Bayley had lived there for many decades. She may wander the back garden still pondering how Mr. Bayley will ever get the boat he built in the carriage house out through its far too narrow doors. That had been a topic of spirited neighborhood conversation for many years. Some think the ghost could even be Hilda Stoughton who lived next door in the Prince House—the old Isaac Sprecher House—who always enjoyed browsing in Mrs. Bayley's beautiful gardens.

One person saw the ghost as a lady in a pink, flowing gown with a matching parasol, walking around the yard at two or three o'clock in the morning as if she had just returned from a great gala ball. That could be any one of those women mentioned. The young son of a professor of music saw her as tall and thin but wearing a long white dress with a beautiful lace collar and bodice. She carried a lacy parasol, walking about in the backyard of Diehl House.

His mother said, "Well, it's probably the professor's wife."

Her son responded, "But, Mother, I can see right through her."

On another occasion, the young man asked his mother, "Who is the pretty lady who holds my hand at night?"

His mother replied, "Are you sure you are not imagining her, my dear? What does she look like?"

Her son again replied, "I see right through her. She plays beautiful music on her piano, but when I go to the piano, there is no one there."

Still a third report was of a lady in a white gown, faceless, standing by the bird feeder or birdbath in the back garden. Still others in the neighborhood associate Diehl House with the specter of a woman who appears walking around the yard as if tending to her garden and occasionally looking out the upstairs window just above the front door as if looking for some delayed but expected caller.

Professor Diehl's final days at Wittenberg apparently were not happy days. He had been ill and had gotten worse. Students were restless in his classes and eager to chuck the ancient languages at the earliest possible opportunity. His wife shared his depression and his monumental unhappiness. In a quarrel with the Board of Directors, he was forced to resign and died within the year. Benjamin Prince in his unpublished history of Wittenberg recorded his view of the matter. Diehl, he wrote, was one of the founders of the school and should have been treated by the Board of Directors with greater Christian charity than he was. Diehl was, he elaborated, "a man of kindly spirit and a friend of everyone." He had been loved and admired by many previous generations of students. He had served with integrity and high moral character and lived a genuine Christian life.

When Diehl's widow gave up their former happy home, it was taken by Ira F. Chorpening, a local business entrepreneur and Treasurer of Wittenberg College. He was heavily involved in local business and in Pennsylvania. The John N. Lyday and Company in Pittsburgh was deeply involved in the very competitive oil boom of that day, and Chorpening was one of the company's major investors. In those wildly speculative ventures, John D. Rockefeller of Cleveland, founder of the Standard Oil Company, was ultimately successful, and Lyday and Company was just one of the early casualties along the way.

The *Springfield Daily Advertiser* reported in January 1867 that a number of Springfield's best men had lost heavily in these oil speculations. Chorpening was one, and his next-door neighbor Isaac Sprecher whom he had talked into the venture was another. How far Wittenberg itself may have gotten involved is unreported. Financial records for the time are nonexistent, and Wittenberg officials denied suffering any great loss, but the school did enter into some very difficult financial times. Samuel Sprecher was constantly on the road, trying to raise badly needed funds.

"I had no idea to what an awful extent things had run," said Chorpening. "By this failure, I utterly ruined my friend Isaac Sprecher."

Isaac Sprecher left Wittenberg for a higher-paying post in Pennsylvania's state education department to recoup his fortune, and he sold his house to the young, up and coming Benjamin Prince. Chorpening resigned as college treasurer and filed for bankruptcy. He moved his wife and seven children further west to start over.

"I am penniless," he wrote a friend, "but have a gift from God in a noble wife."

If one day on a late night or very early in a morning you should see this beautiful lady dancing on the lawns between the Isaac Sprecher and the Diehl Houses, it is not too difficult to imagine that it might be Mrs. Diehl in happier days on one occasion and it is surely Mrs. Chorpening on another. Hilda Stoughton and "Bebe" Bayley cannot be totally discounted either. One day, someone might see the four of them gathering for tea in the garden. If on a late night campus stroll you should see this gentle and lovely apparition in the garden of Diehl House, perhaps you will summon the courage to speak to her. If you are pleasant and genial in your demeanor, perhaps she will tell you her name and explain why she is about at such an hour.

In more recent years, Diehl House had been used as a guesthouse, and more than one guest has reported that the resident ghost, whoever she might be, did not like it when someone occupied her room. She apparently made her displeasure known in the gentlest but nonetheless disturbing ways.

CHAPTER 12

Isaac Sprecher House

HE FIRST KNEW the Isaac Sprecher House in the early 1950s when it was already a century old. If there were a haunted house at Wittenberg, this would be it. Dr. Prince was the longest occupant after Isaac Sprecher before Wittenberg acquired the property from his daughters who had lived there for many, many years. All were now deceased.

When he first saw it, the lot was greatly overgrown with wild shrubbery, unweeded flower beds, high grass, and grotesque, twisted, eerie trees. The weather-beaten old house with its large added-on and ill-fitted front porch was lost somewhere in the midst of that jungle of neglect. During the day, it was an eyesore, easily ignored. At night, it could harbor all manner of wild imaginary beasts.

Some students entered the campus at that southern point, but he and his friends entered from the east side via a narrow path between the Delta Sigma Phi and Phi Mu Delta houses on the west side of Woodlawn Avenue, now Alumni Way. The college acquired the derelict house and lot and began to clear out the overgrowth, making it more presentable while planning for its more glorious future. Its present form gave no hint of its past glory or its planned rebirth as the president's manse.

Isaac Sprecher was the nephew of President Samuel Sprecher. He had come to Wittenberg to study theology but was put immediately to work by his uncle as a college tutor. Eventually, he was advanced to the post of Professor of Ancient Languages and History. In 1857, he built this home at its prime location at the entrance to the campus. The builder was Christopher Thompson, a prominent Springfield stone-and-brick mason who apparently owned the stone quarry at the southwest corner of the campus. The foundation stones for Isaac Sprecher's house, old Wittenberg Hall, Recitation Hall, and other early neighboring houses all came from that quarry. With every stone extracted there came embedded fossils of ancient sea creatures testifying to the geological heritage of this part of Ohio. The practical and fearless Thompson had no truck with phantoms and ghosts and would be only amused by the suggestion that any home he built might be haunted.

In 1878, Isaac Sprecher lost his fortune in oil speculation in Pennsylvania and left Springfield for reasons that we have already explored. He leased the home to Charles F. Ehrenfeld, Professor of English Literature and Latin. He was a Wittenberg alumnus, a Lutheran pastor of the Americanist type, and an abolitionist. And most significantly, he had earned the new PhD—a doctor of philosophy degree—that would become the insignia of the new kind of college professor for whom students yearned, which emerged in late nineteenth-century higher education. His appointment hinted at President Ort's strong intention to bring Wittenberg into the modern age.

Yet in 1883, Ehrenfeld left when Ort became president and the Americanists lost control of the college to more traditional Lutherans. Isaac Sprecher, still in Pennsylvania, then decided he would never be returning to Wittenberg and sold his home to Benjamin Prince. Prince lived there so long that Sprecher and Ehrenfeld were forgotten and the home came to be called The Prince House.

Isaac Sprecher was so forgotten that when his uncle's presidential portrait disappeared, Isaac's portrait was put up in its place and no one was the wiser, even though the two men looked nothing alike. Yet today if you look at the school's incomplete gallery of presidents, it is Isaac not Samuel whose likeness graces that collection. Certainly, if ghosts were discontented souls, Samuel could well be in that category, wandering through the library basement, looking for his lost portrait. When he retired, however, the long white bearded Sprecher—some said he looked like an Albert Durer portrait—moved to California where he started a new Wittenberg-like college with his son-in-law in San Diego. He was far too busy, apparently, to be disturbed by the past.

These first three residents of the Sprecher House—Isaac Sprecher, Charles Ehrenfeld, and Benjamin Prince—successively held the task of collector of student tuitions and fees because of the house's convenient location. Every student at the school for well over half a century went into that house to pay his or her bills.

When ladies were admitted to the college and to its seminary, Benjamin Prince's daughters Flora and Grace became unofficial deans of women. They systematically, it seems, checked out every coed's aspiring beau and reported appropriately to anxious parents. Dating couples—as many alumni later recounted—dutifully accepted an invitation to the Prince House to take tea and play Parcheesi or some other harmless game with the Prince sisters. In what had to be a tense social encounter, such guests endured the Prince sisters' expert and delicate yet prying interrogations. Flora became school librarian in 1892 and served there until 1943, a total of fifty-one years. That left Grace to continue oversight of the coeds' welfare and serve her father as secretary.

Student Lloyd C. Douglas, class of 1900, would later enrich the story of the Sprecher-Prince House more than anyone else. He had entered the Wittenberg Preparatory Academy in 1894. Upperclassmen, he said, stopped him as he crossed the campus to inquire to what class he belonged, just to hear him say "nineteen hundred." When he added that he planned to spend three additional years in seminary, they exclaimed "Nineteen-O-Three" and laughed incredulously. He had great expectations for his future.

"Throughout my childhood and youth," he said, "and during college days, I firmly held an intentional assurance that Destiny would eventually befriend me. Even on dark days, I had that faith. Explain it? No; I can't account for it, but it's the truth."

Later as a novelist, Douglas created something of a phantom Wittenberg, reflecting good and bad ghosts from his own memory of his student days at Wittenberg. Give them another half century and they will be the long-forgotten roots of new ghosts in the Isaac Sprecher House. In *Forgive Us Our Trespasses*, he created a President Goldthwaite to preside over Magnolia College. His fictional man was an amalgam of Wittenberg's genial sixth President Charles G. Heckert and the more brusque Benjamin Prince, both of whom he had known as a student, and an irascible Rees Edgar Tulloss with whom he wrestled long and hard as an alumnus. The argument became so vehement that, it was said, he wrote Wittenberg out of his will. It was all over a question of his repayment of a student loan which by custom was forgiven when the student was ordained. When he left the ministry to become a novelist, Tulloss thought he should repay the loan. Douglas said that he had promised to be in full-time Christian service. "I am," he argued; "Even as a novelist, I am fulfilling my promise." The dollar amount involved was minimal in current dollars. Apparently, for both men, it was the principle of it all. The file in the archives of the college covering the dispute is nearly a foot thick.

Douglas captured the function of a president's house well in describing the events in Goldthwaite's house at Magnolia College. His novel may well have been the source of President Stoughton's later vision of that house as the Wittenberg president's manse. Douglas may have implied by the school's fictitious name that it was a sleepy, out-of-the-way kind of southern place, off America's beaten path. But Goldthwaite entertained men of wealth and their wives. He and his gracious wife hosted college board members and community and church leaders. He spent hours with members of the faculty who had complaints, suggestions, or helpful plans to advance their school or themselves, or both, or who just needed to be comforted or reassured, and faculty wives who may have expected at lot more from marrying a college professor than they got. Most of all, he entertained lots of students whose attitudes toward the encounter ranged from fear that they had been "found out" in some indiscretion to the haughty outlook of many talented youth, like Douglas himself, who believed they actually deserved all the president's time that he so willingly showered upon them.

Surprisingly, Goldthwaite spent an inordinate amount of time with students who felt like "outsiders;" those not selected to join a college fraternity or sorority because they didn't want to or they weren't wanted. Sherwood Anderson, another Wittenberg author, went through "rush" but decided he was in too big a hurry to get into the world of business—a great mistake as it turned out—to waste all that time at the Beta house or completing his degree. Goldthwaite held a great just-before-Thanksgiving-breakfast for all the unaffiliated. Heckert was a Beta, as was Prince, and Tulloss was a Phi Psi. Douglas himself was a Phi Gamma Delta, at the time the youngest of the Greek societies. His ardor faded as he got older. But Goldthwaite recognized the growing number of so-called barbarians who cast their lot as unaffiliated independents. There was a great rivalry between the "ins" and the "outs" that grew in the roaring twenties, and Douglas recorded it.

Douglas said the book was a story about how forgiveness or the lack of it can completely change the way you look at life. He had probably not forgotten that that was the advice that the genial Dean Shatzer gave to every student in school. "We should all," Dean Shatzer said, "be more accepting of the differences we find among us." Douglass was surprised at how well this and all his other books had sold. He said they were "clumsy pieces of work" where all the characters were decent and everything turned out happily at the end. He wished that for every student everywhere.

Douglas had trained for the ministry but became in his day a very celebrated novelist. He wrote *The Robe*, a biblical blockbuster about the crucifixion; *The Big Fisherman*, a best seller on the life of Simon Peter; and *Magnificent Obsession* that was about a family doctor who saved lives and souls. All three novels were made into smash movies of their day, rerun later on television for over a decade. More than likely, phantoms of his own college acquaintances live on in these stories; certainly the buildings do. The historic Wittenberg Circle, old Wittenberg Hall, the hill of the wise men, and the Prince House figure prominently in a fourth novel, *Forgive Our Trespasses*. In older and grumpier days, Douglas revisited his college days a second time in a memoir entitled *A Time to Remember*.

Behind Douglas's memories and his long-running battle with President Tulloss, and greatly complicating his view of matters, was a haunting recollection of his father's own unsuccessful adventure at Wittenberg. He said he loved his father with a devotion akin to worship. He was, he said in his reminiscences, the acknowledged protégé of his father. The chain of events, his father being at Wittenberg in the 1850s, the son being there in the 1900s, and the writing of the son's novels in 1950s, cover a century in time that was very influential in the novelist's growth and development.

Alexander Jackson Douglas, the son related, enrolled with a friend during Samuel Sprecher's earliest years. He was at first quite impressed by Dr. Sprecher whose theology, he said, was focused on the "symbolism of the Bible" and did not put such a strain upon a reasonable man's mind. He all but worshipped Dr. Sprecher, said the son, and he went to work for Sprecher as his man Friday. He was Sprecher's "hosteller," taking care of his guests. He was coachman, gardener, dishwasher, and errand boy, said the son. His father, he said, saw Sprecher as "warm-hearted, a scholar and a seer, his idol and his hero." Yet Alexander Jackson Douglas is not listed anywhere as ever having been a student or as an alumnus of Wittenberg or at its School of Theology. The novelist said that his father ended his days at Wittenberg in a great theological dispute with the Examining Committee over infant baptism, the existence of the Devil, and Martin Luther's unnecessary belligerence, not to mention the proper deference a youthful candidate should display toward an Examining Committee.

All these experiences and embellishments make the story of a haunted Isaac Sprecher House more complicated. A number of former Wittenbergers tell their own stories. One, a successful professional artist used to exploring her feelings and emotions related an experience in the house, going up stairs. "The hairs," she said, "stood up on the back of my head and neck. I sensed a presence that I neither saw nor heard, but felt I was not alone."

A development officer responsible for raising funds for Wittenberg stayed one night in the northwest bedroom that had been Benjamin Prince's room from which he could see the entire campus. "Ezra Keller," he said, "grasped me tightly by the upper arms and told me what I needed to do for Wittenberg." The next morning, I woke up with bruises on my arms, but I did not tell anyone at the time." I find it difficult to imagine Dr. Keller in a building that was not there until after he had died. But then we are not talking about reason or logic when we talk about such things as these.

Then there was President Kinnison's family dog Bonaparte—half dachshund and half French poodle—who danced about on his hind legs, looking up at the second floor landing, growling and barking at someone or something that no one else could see.

CHAPTER 13

Flying Dutchmen Everywhere

FOR WHATEVER REASONS, several generations of Wittenberg students from 1863 to 1883—believers in ghosts and nonbelievers—organized their lives for several student generations as passengers on that ghost ship called *The Flying Dutchman*. It was this historic episode that prompted the first ghost storywriter to name his ghost *The Flying Dutchman*. These students did not have to tell a ghost story, they became the ghost story, the fantasy that changed Wittenberg College forever. It was probably the longest sustained metaphor in college journalism since its emergence on the nineteenth-century campus. It hypnotized Wittenberg students for two decades. They sailed in and out of Springfield, Ohio and all the way to Hawaii and back as phantoms agitating for reform of the college curriculum, campus rules and regulations, and student lifestyles. They agitated for coeducation, independent student publications, and Greek letter societies.

The basic legend of a phantom ship in the 1840s was that of a doomed ship sailing around the Cape of Good Hope at the bottom of the earth and bringing misfortune to any other ship that crossed its path. In another version, *The Flying Dutchman* was captained by one Hendrick Van der Decken of the Netherlands who was returning home to Amsterdam. A terrible storm blew up, but Van der Decken would not wait for it to die down. He cursed God and the elements and vowed to sail until doomsday under his own authority. For this blasphemy, he was condemned to sail on forever, unable to reach any harbor until he begged for forgiveness. Alas, his hapless crew—at Wittenberg, the students—was condemned to sail on forever with him.

Students had learned of the legend in various ways and accepted it almost immediately as a metaphor for Wittenberg's situation as they saw it. In 1839, Frederick Marryat published a novel *The Phantom Ship* that they might have seen. A German author, Heinrich Heine, romanticized the story, allowing his captain to go ashore every seven years and regain his freedom if he could win the heart of an unsullied maiden. In 1843, Richard Wagner, a German composer, set the romantic story to music in his opera *Der fliegende Holländer* which became popular in Europe and America.

By the 1860s, the legend was quite well known. In the popular form best known to students at Wittenberg, a stubborn German ship captain, like their own professor Hezekiah Reubush Geiger, commanded. Geiger was Wittenberg's chief operating officer, while President Sprecher attended to academic affairs and financial planning. The crew, which they imagined were the Wittenberg students, begged him to head for a safe harbor. Geiger stubbornly refused. He defied fate, even daring God to sink his fragile ship rather than accept any plan to bring his school into the modern world. In his punishment, he and his fellow officers—the rest of the faculty—were condemned to sail forever in an increasingly obsolete ship through increasingly turbulent waters. The students, his unfortunate and tormented crew, were all condemned to die with them. But the students, then still all male, were optimistic about their future and believed they would be rescued in the end by that beautiful maiden. They received great support and advice from a local newspaper editor, Clifton M. Nichols, who was a strong advocate of a thorough reform of American higher education and believed Wittenberg would be a good place to start.

For two and a half decades, students collectively called for change. They founded secret societies like Phi Kappa Psi and Beta Theta Pi to separate themselves into smaller groups beyond the eye and control of faculty as enrollment grew. They hosted guest speakers who talked about the coming "new woman" and the benefits of coeducation. They published underground newspapers called *The Flying Dutchman* to express their ideas anonymously and freely and made an assault on the board and faculty's authority over their lives, on a narrow and

WILLIAM A. KINNISON

restricted course of study, and on an overly pietistic campus atmosphere. They wanted more useful modern languages, modern literature, public speaking, art, music, drama, economics and political science, more pure science, and more advanced mathematics. Eventually, they also wanted intercollegiate sports and to identify themselves with American college students everywhere.

In 1863, as one student described it, "a new planet, a star of the first magnitude flashed across the heavens to the alarm of the faculty. This was none other than the *The Flying Dutchman.*" It commented on less well-liked students, especially those who sided with the authorities against their own generation. Editor Nichols noted the student paper's appearance: "*The Flying Dutchman* flew over the city yesterday morning and knocked over several gentlemen by brushing them with his wings and tail." He was the first to write of the phantom ship as if it were a great giant bird. "A package of money and several bouquets," he added, "have been left with us for the editor of *The Flying Dutchman.*"

Students at Wittenberg and elsewhere distributed underground papers during the final two weeks of the school year. At Wittenberg, where students persisted with underground papers longer than those at most schools, the paper appeared on alumni weekend and was available through final examinations, the annual meeting of the board of directors at which diplomas were approved or disapproved, and the graduation ceremony when degrees were awarded. It was the fortnight when all the powers in the school's universe were gathered together, when the most people would see it, and when there was very little time left in which to discover the culprits—always seniors about to graduate.

In 1863, it was the *Flying Dutchman*; in 1866, the *Flying Dutchman's Pap.* One student noted, "The ancestor proved worse than its offspring." With the second appearance of the paper, the faculty decided it needed to do more than it had done earlier to find the culprits and call them to account. This edition was more scurrilous and represented a growing rebelliousness. The rumor among overly excited students was that the faculty had offered a $50.00 reward for the offenders, "dead or alive," as if they were western desperados. The sum equaled nearly a full year's expenses for tuition, fees, and books. Noting faculty displeasure, more traditional students called an indignation meeting and passed resolutions condemning the paper as the act of "misguided persons." What was meant as "a mere sally of wit on the faculty and students" had gone too far, becoming "slander, vulgarity, and profanity." They issued a notice "to show to the public our entire disapprobation of the character of the paper and of the misdirected effort of those who endeavored to create a little sport at the expense of all that is good and pure."

The offenders included a good proportion of the senior class and many senior members of the fraternities. The chief culprit that year, the editor and publisher, Joshua Shaffer, a nonfraternity man and the roommate of our very helpful and persistent student diarist George Settlemyer. A committee of the board had, as was its custom, examined the seniors on their academic capacities earlier and was prepared to make its customary recommendation that "the gentlemen be graduated." This time, however, their motion was tabled pending a further discussion of the "editing and publishing of a certain paper known as the *Flying Dutchman's Pap*." The board satisfied itself that Shaffer was responsible, and he was summoned to the board's session at 7:30 a.m., commencement morning. Sprecher and board member Samuel Bowman, an alumnus and a lawyer, cross-examined him.

Shaffer ventured alone into the room with the rest of the senior class nervously awaiting the outcome, their degrees perhaps hanging in the balance. It was a subdued Joshua Shaffer who, as class sacrificial lamb, confessed responsibility. His task was to placate the board without implicating anyone else and then, if possible, to extricate himself. Such was his winsome personality that he succeeded beyond all expectations. The board decided that Shaffer could graduate if he made a written apology expressing penitence and a promise to avoid slanderous and scandalous publications in the future. When he had complied, the motion that "the gentlemen be graduated" was removed from the table and passed. The board adjourned just in time for the exercises to begin, much to everyone's relief.

One of the onerous tasks that students had hoped to have eliminated was the oration that every one of them had to give at commencement to demonstrate publicly their level of accomplishment. Shaffer had so impressed the board that they allowed him to speak. His oration was entitled "The Importance of True Ideals." A reporter at commencement noted the exuberance with which the audience greeted him. His appearance "at the front, whether from his good looks or some other source, was stoutly applauded." The class saluted its hero. Shaffer urged the class to pursue what might be before settling for what already was. Some years later, Joshua Shaffer returned to campus as a duly elected member of the board of directors.

But that was not the end of the *Flying Dutchman*. In 1870 another edition, the *Flying Dutchman's Granddaddy*, was even more venomous. The editor was a senior who had prepared as his graduation oration a legitimate address on "The Coming Woman" which was a critique of the faculty and board for not as yet having admitted women students. While his address was a straightforward defense of the emerging American woman and her right to a college education and fairer treatment in society, his article in the *Granddaddy* was something else. The senior had craftily written about his coming speech with double entendres and several vulgar suggestions. Thus, as he would deliver his serious address at commencement, many in the audience would be convulsed by remembering the suggestive references in the *Dutchman*. He was caught before the day of commencement and was required to sign a retraction of his statements. He was also denied the opportunity to address the assembly and was denied graduation. In protest, another student refused to accept his degree when his name was called. No happy or heroic ending this time.

A fourth edition of the *Flying Dutchman,* the *Flying Dutchman's Grand Mammy,* appeared in June of 1872. It was extremely personal in its references to faculty and continued to harass members of board, faculty, and student body most unpopular with the anonymous reporters. In this paper, where complimentary references to Editor "Cliff" Nichols boldly appeared, the assault on the faculty was stronger than ever. The student editors took pains, as they always did, to exempt Dr. Sprecher from the criticisms: "He is an example of the true scholar. His taste for study would inspire any young man." Students were eager to be in his classes, the article continued, and they attended with both profit and pleasure. No one else escaped a scathing review. The prejudices expressed reflected Editor Nichols' own view: profound respect for Dr. Sprecher, disdain for the rest.

After several more editions of a better or worse *Dutchman,* some students finally moved in a new direction: an annual book of college memories. The underground papers continued for a while longer, but a new voice for students had begun. Naming the school's first yearbook *The Aloha* was an historical act. It tied the new publication to the tradition of the previous *Flying Dutchmen* as the captain Professor Geiger sailed into port in Hawaii, seeking redemption, just as the real professor on leave from campus actually sailed into that very port.

This new editorial venture sought to put an end to that long-extended metaphor that had existed since 1863. The good ship *Flying Dutchman* finally put in at the Cannibal Islands, the Sandwich Islands, the Hawaiian Islands bearing none other than Prof. Hezekiah Geiger, just before he resigned his position at the college. He was met with the traditional greeting "Aloha." The editors also stepped off the *Flying Dutchman* onto the shore holding a large sign that read, "An organ of this nature has long been desired by the advocates of student rights and former efforts have bubbled forth in the mysterious and troublesome *Dutchman."* Its stated mission was to review Wittenberg as the students see it and to "reveal to the world student life as it really is" not as the authorities wished it to be or what they hoped others would think it to be. The new yearbook was thus given that exotic title, explaining why in its introduction and attempting to write "finis" to a seventeen-year long story.

In June of 1882, as a new, reforming president Samuel Ort had been selected, students finally issued a new underground paper, this time not another *Dutchman.* They called it the *Collegian.* It saluted new president Samuel Alfred Ort and his decision to keep Wittenberg in Springfield and celebrated Springfield as the perfect place for this school to be. It bade farewell to Prof. Geiger and his fellow Flying Dutchmen and saluted their new officers—modern, university-trained college professors with earned doctorates bringing a modern curriculum and greater latitude in student life.

At Ort's inauguration, citizens of the town and nearly every living alumnus of the college were present with a deep sense of crisis and doom because the struggle between the past and the future had been so great. "Now of all times," many said, "Wittenbergers should stand together." Ort had been a *Philosophian* in college, but was very aware of the *Excelsior Society's* prophecy: "If it is right to conceive of a time when Wittenberg's faculty and authorities would forget the origins and destiny of the institution and let it fail, there are those gone out from the *Excelsior Society* who would gather at the grave of the sainted Dr. Keller and catching the echoes of the hymn which rose when its foundations were laid, would establish Wittenberg anew." Ort's life had been a clear example of "Excelsiorism"—getting things done—a spirit that was personified also in the growing enthusiasm of the school's alumni.

It had not been "a blunder to have founded Wittenberg in Springfield," said the new president. Wittenberg would continue to educate students to "lift mankind to the higher plane." There would be "no controversy with science" and no debate with "practical education" but Wittenberg would not lose sight of "the truth that man has within him which craves more than just the bread he eats." The nation needed colleges s like Wittenberg, he added. "We plead for Wittenberg because she has a right to live" and to "become the institution she was conceived to be from her beginning." It was as if he were fulfilling the prophecy in their very presence, renewing the institution's reason for being.

One wonders if that *Excelsior* host and other like-minded alumni were now among the restless spirits gathered quietly that day after some very busy days preceding Ort's selection. They peered out the windows of Old Wittenberg Hall and from behind the trees and shrubs of the hill of the wise.

By calling their new paper the *Collegian* rather than another edition of the *Flying Dutchman*, students signaled an important change in their view of themselves and of their school. They were part of a new self-conscious national class of students with unique institutions. There were many indications that Wittenberg was finding a place in the emerging system of higher education as an identifiable type: a residential, undergraduate, liberal arts college. Students were thinking of themselves not as students at a uniquely different evangelical Lutheran college but as collegians on a challenging American campus.

Wittenberg's inclusion on the list of Ohio's top colleges was one example. A growing Greek-letter system with local chapters of national organizations, they thought, was another. Coeducation was still another very important step. Growing interest in intercollegiate sports and collegiate fads in clothing and behavior were other manifestations soon to follow. As Dr. Ort saw it, it meant saving the best of the past and combining it with the best of the future as God gave them the capacity to determine it.

One distinction went unmentioned even as the spirits of the past swirled about the changing campus: Wittenberg as America's most haunted campus.

CHAPTER 14

The Disappearing Rock
of the Class of 1874

IT WAS A large, heavy, granite-like, oval-shaped stone, at least six feet wide, four or so feet high, and five feet deep. Whether it came out of the hole when they dug the basement of Wittenberg Hall or was a rejected stone hauled up the hill for the foundation or whether it rolled there later by mysterious powers possessed by the students in the class of 1874 is not known. In any event, after the class first organized in the fall of 1870, they seized upon this rock lying just off the southwest corner of the steps to the hall entrance as the emblem of their class. They appeared to have been the first class to select a physical object to make certain that they would not be forgotten. They claimed that as freshmen, they had struggled manfully to roll it up the hill, like Sisyphus himself, to occupy its commanding position. They hired a stone mason to carve five-inch-high numerals 1, 8, 7, and 4 on the stone and declared their intention to mark their class as the most outstanding class at Wittenberg of all time. They shortened the inscription to the numbers 7 and 4, only because the mason charged by the letter and that was all they could afford. This took place fifty years before the columned portico adorned the hall. The rock is clearly visible in an oil painting by A. Linaweaver, a member of the class.

Their initiative inspired subsequent classes. The class of 1875 made its mark by planting a tree near the hall's entrance, though it died within a few years. The campus had remained forested, however, because of the many, many classes who planted trees. The class of 1876 carved its numerals on the face of the stones of the massive steps to the first floor. In European fashion, the first floor was called the ground floor and the second the first. The class of 1877 purchased a marble slab and had it set into the wall at the side of the front entrance, with a Greek motto that in English meant "Prosperity Consists in Action." This school of the West placed great emphasis on that idea of Ralph Waldo Emerson, a nineteenth-century American philosopher, that scholarship should lead to action, activity, and achievement, getting something done because of one's learning; Excelsior—ever upward and onward.

There were fifteen men in the graduating class, but Linaweaver, the student who had painted the picture of the hall with the rock, was not listed among them because he had withdrawn from school. The year 1874 had been crucial in the school's life and one well worth remembering. At the June 1874 meeting of the Board of Directors, at President Sprecher's suggestion, the board voted to outlaw Greek-letter societies, to admit African American students as a result of the passage of the Civil Rights Act by Congress, to enroll female students, and to accept the president's resignation. Bowing, Sprecher thought, to campus desire for a modern president, he proposed to remain as a professor in the seminary. He remained for ten more years and then retired and surprised all by moving to California. Professor Geiger was certain that he should be the next president, but surprisingly, he was not selected, and a red-headed board member John B. Helwig was. That too was a surprise because he was not the reformer everyone expected but another stalwart of the founders. He was not a professor either. The class of 1874 would be one of the last graduating classes comprised entirely of men. Amid it all, Professor Geiger became a very disgruntled man.

More mysterious than the tale of how the rock of the class of 1874 got there, however, is the story of its disappearance and where it might have gone. The great rock stood in place for 120 years without desecration. No other class had captured it for its own glorification or even tried to do so as far as we know. It had been honored by every class since 1874, reposing in place.

No one apparently even noticed for months that it was gone. Without fanfare, someone or some group, whether in the dead of night or in broad daylight, quietly and surreptitiously stole away with it. The rock vanished sometime after 1995. Living witnesses testified to its presence at least until that year. Spirits of the long-deceased class of '74 were reportedly extremely depressed and confused by their rock's disappearance and by the callous disrespect for a class memorial that the act demonstrated. It had become not merely a memorial to their class but a monument to coeducation, to a more diverse student body, and to the beginning of modern Wittenberg. Perhaps they exaggerated its importance, but that is what classes do in youthful celebration. What did its disappearance mean? It was as if the entire class had been obliterated from Wittenberg's memory as though they had never existed. It was an affront that no class could possibly tolerate, and they thought collectively about revenge. Maybe they could put a horse in the cupola or roll a huge boulder down the hallway late at night or remove all the pews from the chapel.

Some believed that the rock had just rolled down the hill one summer evening when school was out of session. They said it came to rest just above a beautiful reconfiguration of the once rustic Commencement Hollow where the old college brook had crept along for so many years under what they now called Kissing Bridge then on to Lagonda Creek. Discovered there one morning, toppled over so as to hide the numerals 7 and 4, the stone was scrubbed and polished and inscribed with an abbreviation of the college motto: "Pass It On." A few years later, that was effaced, and a large W took its place.

A more rational explanation was that the school's business manager was asked by a new president, eager to "dress things up," to find a big rock to place between Recitation Hall and the entrance to the nicely remodeled Commencement Hollow. The spirits of the offended class were no more pleased with this rationalization than any other. They preferred to believe that on a dark and deserted night, evil men had deliberately rolled the class memorial down the hill of wise men, stealing it for their own purposes when another rock could have been procured fairly easily and at very little cost. No one, these cynical men believed, would even miss the rock at its old location, and surely no member of the class of 1874 would be heard from.

To the contrary, the fifteen ghosts of the class of 1874 and A. Linaweaver and others who had dropped out before graduating were insistent upon being heard. They believed they needed to warn all other classes and those yet to come of the outrage they had had to endure and to tell them that they should be wary of any institutional commitment that they would be honored forever by their alma mater. They thought that they might hide in the shrubbery in Commencement Hollow for every graduation and heckle the new class with their warning. But leery of such a long commitment, they decided instead to put a curse on such mornings for bad, cold, rainy, and windy weather.

But certainly you would say that the troubled class of 1874 presumed to have more power over that day's weather than they are actually entitled to. We cannot forget the angry Shawnee woman at the spring and the beautiful maiden who strolls along the bed of the now dried up old brook and who also cast spells for rain on that special day. All three together, however, provide a triple ghostly power that considerably reduces the odds of a dry commencement day ever.

WILLIAM A. KINNISON

CHAPTER 15

Another Unlucky Room

THE ROOMS IN Wittenberg Hall were all more or less alike—some larger for three or four men, others slightly smaller for two occupants or one. The rooms were quadrangles of generous size with high ceilings. On the south side of the building, the rooms all had one large window overlooking the Wittenberg hill, the campus entrance, and Springfield off in the distance. On the north side, across a wide hallway, the rooms had one window overlooking the community pump, the cistern, and the students' fuel supplies of wood or coal, the hollow behind, and to the east, Dr. Sprecher's home. On the ridge beyond the hollow was Woodshade Cemetery. There were desks at the large window and bunk beds or singles in two of the four corners, with a potbellied stove in another corner, expelling its smoke up narrow pipes to stacks on the roof. Central heating and plumbing did not arrive until the turn of the century.

William and Joshua shared a room on the north side of the hallway on the third floor not far from the eastern stairwell. Joshua sat at his desk, daydreaming. His eyes often wandered through the old cemetery in the distance. They were upperclassmen with reasonably good grades, progressing steadily, if not with distinction, toward graduation two years hence. William was studying the sciences, while Joshua followed the more traditional humanities course and planned to enter the seminary. William was not inclined toward physical exertion, while a long walk in the woods was, for Joshua, the most inspiring and rigorous part of his day. The two thus pursued divergent enough paths that they could argue quite extensively on any number of topics and stretch the tolerance of their intellectual boundaries. That presumably was the philosophical justification of sharing rooms with strangers and for dormitory living in general. They expanded their understanding of individual differences and learned to live in a world of widely different ideas and differing sorts of people, some more agreeable than others.

Nevertheless, Joshua did not want to share his latest nightmare with his roommate because he was of such a scientific bent and would be quite intolerant of any emotionalism, as he called it, that Joshua was likely to express. William, he feared, probably did not believe in dreams and certainly did not consider them of any significance. He did not accept modern psychology as scientific. He wanted to keep his senses sharp and not subject to any romantic delusions such as dreams, fantasies, and phantoms. Joshua's fantasy, as he was sure William would call it, was merely the result of a stomach troubled by a piece of rotten potato. "Therefore, please," Joshua insisted to a student from next door, "let me tell you my experience while William is out of the room."

In the middle of the night, Joshua began, he had awakened to see the wildest and most horrible face—a strange-looking man smoking a long-stemmed pipe, with a long white beard, wearing a three-cornered hat, staring in his third-floor window. Whether it was a prehistoric savage or the whimsical Flying Dutchman Joshua had heard about, he did not know. He was stunned into silence at the very sight of someone staring at him through a window thirty-some feet above ground level. He sat motionless for what seemed like an hour, not even noticing for the longest time that William was not in his bed.

Suddenly, Joshua and his neighbor heard a loud crash of some metallic object bouncing off the hallway walls and clattering down the open stairwell to the floor below. His roommate burst into the room, breathless and speechless, slamming the door behind him, his scientific reserve sorely assaulted by emotions beyond his control. He thought he had heard a rat in the hall, he said, so taking a candle stand, he had gone into the hallway to see. It took him hours, it seemed, well into the morning before he could finish his story with any semblance of cohesion.

Joshua and his neighbor finally deduced that, rather than finding a rat, William had seen a scantily dressed Native American with a spear in his hand, creeping up the stairs and into the third-floor hallway.

WILLIAM A. KINNISON

Perhaps the phantom planned to continue up to the next floor, but William had attracted his attention. He said he thrust his candle stand at the creature, and his hand and the stand passed right through him. Joshua very carefully and slowly asked him so as not to upset him if the two of them might have had a shared dream in which they each might have had different aspects of the same nightmare, even though they had had different suppers and could not have shared the same dyspepsia. He was quite proud of his composure, the calm logic of his question, and the clarity with which he spoke it. William just stared at him and the neighbor as if he did not understand a word that he had uttered or, worse, as if he had been muttering incoherently.

Now combining his story with William's, Joshua feared that they had actually been under assault by an ancient race coming at them from inside and outside the hall and would have liked to have heard William's reasoned view of the matter. William never answered but stared silently at the ceiling. He left immediately at daybreak, never returning to his room in Wittenberg Hall ever again. Joshua received a letter from William a week later, asking him to ship all his worldly goods that he had left behind to him at his home.

In a note that Joshua attached to the smallest of the parcels, he urged William to return and face his fears. He assured him that their extreme event was merely part of the testing to which they were all subjected in their common living experience. He reminded him of how Job was tested in the Old Testament. "Thou scarest me with dreams," Job had said to God, "and terrifiest me through visions." William made no response, and Joshua neither saw nor heard from him ever again.

Subsequently, Joshua had a dream about the ever-changing world at Wittenberg and pondered whether to write his former roommate to tell him about it. It was about an "old boy," an alumnus, who had returned for a campus visit. The visitor had wandered aimlessly through the campus and saw a hundred ghosts and specters and a crowd of students he used to know. As he thought about it, he decided that this was probably not the basis on which he should try to revive William's former connection to Wittenberg Hall or their long conversations over this and that.

CHAPTER 16

The Campus Circle

Adapted from a story in the *Wittenberger* Vol.
XXV no. 7, November 5, 1898

I HAVE ALWAYS been delighted to sit in a dark room or to lie at night on my bunk and muse on pleasures and events that can never happen. I love to let my imagination go unrestrained while I remain quiet and inactive, following the phantoms that pass before me in my mind's eye. Thus, when I was approached by a professor and was asked to guard one of the college buildings on Halloween, I consented willingly, thinking it was not a task but a pleasure. I wondered why this professor was so anxious to have the building guarded and asked one of the older students about it. He told me that ever since the class of 1895 greased all the chairs in the recitation rooms on Halloween in 1894, the college authorities had thought it best to guard "Reci," our nickname for the building, on that evening of wayward goblins.

We were all anticipating the approaching turn of the century, leaving behind the old nineteenth century and venturing into a great new modern age. Professor of English Charles Heckert, soon to be elected president, a member of the *Excelsior Society*, urged us not to be alarmed about the changes to come. The judgments and policies of our fathers would be "peremptorily banished to the limbo of things that were good enough for their day, but not ours," he said. The demand of the new age, he urged, was for all things modern. In that climate, none of us actually believed in the witches or goblins I am about to describe. We celebrated them at Halloween as myths and great fun, forgetting the evils and cruelty of the witch-burnings of New England and Europe centuries before. To our discredit, we referred to modern witches with humor and rollicking laughter.

Just after sundown, I entered the building. There was a good fire in the furnace, so I entered the girls' "gab room" and took my seat before the register. The "gab room" was the women students' lounge and retreat, located next door to the president's classroom and office, where they could escape the constant attention of their male classmates. The name was given by the boys based on the sounds they heard when loitering outside the door. The name was much resented by the lady students. Their room, they complained, "has been barbarously named." It was "an unjust imposition" and gave an image that was "totally devoid of justice and wholly inappropriate for a place so comprehensive and important." The women's literary club, the *Hesperian Society,* declared, "A college without girls is only half blessed; it is an orchard without blossoms, and a spring without song."

I enjoyed my musings in the ladies' sanctuary for some time, the solitude being enlivened by the noise of falling stones and the stacking of rooms in the dormitory on the hill. Students often on Halloween "stacked" a room by filling it with chairs from wall to wall and from floor to ceiling and all the way to the door. It was a real puzzle deciding where to start to unstack a room once it was fully stacked. In such events in past years, they had gotten chairs from all over the campus, and it was a ferocious chore to get them back where they had come from. If truth were told, they never did, and all classrooms had long since become a random assortment of mismatched chairs. It is doubtful that anyone can now sort them out. So far on my night watch, there had been no attempt to break into Reci for chairs.

The moon rose in the east with all the splendor of an oriental queen, and as I peered into the chilly autumn night, my thoughts wandered back to the time when witches, elves, and ghosts inhabited the earth on Halloween. I thought of the adventures of the startled peasants of medieval Europe that we had talked about in class; the stories that the old serfs repeated around the fire on winter evenings; and the primitive desires to destroy that which they did not understand. I could see Tam o'Shanter pursued by the witches, hastening for a nearby sacred brook and escape. I thought of the stormy, windy weather when the wind sighed and moaned through the ancient woods where every sound was interpreted as the voice of a supernatural being and where every shadow in those ancient days was mistaken for a witch.

About midnight, I heard someone walking on the circular drive that ran past Recitation Hall. The road was first marked out by the wagons delivering limestone foundation stones and bricks to build the first college building over half a century ago. I was on the alert. I quietly crouched in the shadow of the curtain and gazed cautiously out onto the campus. But there was no danger; the passerby was only a theology student returning to "the angel factory" from a visit to a friend in town. The noise in the dormitory had ceased, and the only sound that could be heard was the blowing of the wind and the crackling of the dry leaves still on the trees. It was beginning to get cold, so I descended to the basement and stirred up the fire. In the course of about half an hour, the "gab room" was again as cozy as I could wish, so I lay down on the study table, intending to enjoy my thoughts.

But being all alone in a large building is not as pleasant as it might at first seem to a contemplative student seeking peace and quiet for reflection. I became tired of my musings and, in the room's warmth, dozed off. I caught myself at it and aroused myself, but after a while, I succumbed entirely, and in a few moments, I was fast asleep. In my slumber, I had a great dream. I thought that I was on duty, guarding a college building, when suddenly, I saw a very old woman with a broomstick, scolding me with many gestures, but I could not make out a word that she was saying. At the same time, I was in a little hut, and there were several peasants around me. It was a very stormy night; the wind was blowing a hurricane, and the rain was falling in torrents. The old woman turned away from me and, straddling the broomstick, flew away. But in a few moments, she returned with many other witches carrying a boardwalk of the type commonly in use on mud-prone parts of our footpaths. I recognized the walk as belonging to the campus and shouted to them not to carry it away. They dropped it, causing a great noise, and I awoke with a start.

WILLIAM A. KINNISON

With a sensation of pleasure that it was only a dream and a feeling of foolishness that my imagination could carry me to such nonsensical heights, I looked out of the window when, to my great surprise, I noticed several people carrying a boardwalk just as it had occurred in my dream. They walked hastily across the campus toward Buck Creek. I quickly raised the window and shouted at them, but it was as if they did not hear me. They did not look around or answer but stumbled on at a steady pace. I attempted to follow but lost track of them in the brush that covered the top of the cliffs. I had begun to retrace my steps to the warm room I had left, when I noticed a bright red glow across the way in one of the dormered attic windows in the ladies' residence, Ferncliff Hall. It was the area of the building set aside as the women's gymnasium where they exercised and pursued physical education. Just like the men's gym, it was often used "after hours" for a multitude of spontaneous student activities.

The light in the window was so bright and flickered so rapidly that I thought that the building was on fire. I started to run for the recently installed alarm box a block away when, through the window, I saw several coeds dancing around in the red glare of the light. Expecting any moment to see a terror-stricken maiden cast herself from the attic window onto the cold, hard earth below, I stood, trembling, waiting for the worst. But the expected did not happen, and at second look, I noticed the girls were laughing and smiling, having a wonderful time in a ghostly parade around a brightly burning orange-red light. With a sigh of relief, I witnessed the scene as the girls marched up and down past the window. I wondered why it was that girls should indulge in such giddy pranks in the middle of the night, just like some of the antics of the men.

Philosophizing on the folly of all mankind and perplexed about the whereabouts of the boardwalk that probably came from one of our professor's houses, I returned to Recitation Hall. All was silent, and I sat quietly for four more hours, thinking on the witches and ghosts whom I had seen in my dreams and about the ladies in Ferncliff Hall, trying to arrive at some conclusion on the reality of it all. I was not sure whether I had been asleep or awake or what was real or unreal. But at six o'clock in the morning, I went up to the seminary where the boardwalk belonged. It was gone, actually gone. I had also heard that there was a little round hole burned in the floor of the attic room where the ladies' gym was located. I was told that a pair of rubber shoes was placed carefully over the spot so that no one would notice it, but they did not quite cover it. No one could be found who knew anything about how any of this occurred, and the boardwalk was never found.

As I pondered the unusual event in the ladies' gym in the attic of Ferncliff Hall, I recalled rumors of recent years of some of the lady students attempting to establish a strange new society they whispered about—a fraternity for women. When women first enrolled, many were hopeful, I am told, that they might join the men's literary societies. In anticipation of that revolutionary idea, there was a dubious rumor that the proactive *Excelsiors* had invited the reclusive American woman poet Emily Dickinson to accept honorary membership in their society. To their delight, some claimed, she actually accepted and wrote, expressing her appreciation. Alas, the faculty decided that the women should have their own separate organizations. The idea of women debating the social and political issues of the day with men in public was just too revolutionary. The ladies succeeded in forming a group of their own.

They also began asking members of the men's Greek-letter fraternities curious questions about their mysterious new secret societies. It was difficult for some of us to maintain our oaths of secrecy, taken on pain of death, not to reveal what it was that the girls most wanted to know. Not for another four years would they succeed in establishing their sorority, yet they certainly were making progress if the session in the ladies' gym on Halloween in 1898 was any indication. If campus rumor was to be credited, that mysterious event was an early effort at the establishment of an initiation ritual for just what those modern ladies wanted—a fraternity for women.

As the witches in Shakespeare's *Macbeth* chanted,

When shall we three meet again?
In thunder, lightning, or in rain?
When the hurly-burly's done,
When the battle's lost and won.
That will be ere set of sun.
Where the place?

Why, Wittenberg, of course.

CHAPTER 17

The Red Velvet Chair

I T WAS AT first just a rumor. A little tale quietly tattled among friends in an ever-widening, even though small, circle. It took some weeks for it to come to his attention, and at first, he did not take it very seriously. It was only of interest to a few alumni of our little college and attracted little attention at all among those outside that circle.

The rumor was that Wittenberg was possessed of a haunted chair, perhaps even more than one. No, not a haunted chair of history or a haunted chair of modern literature; it was an actual chair—a fancy, carved and upholstered wooden Victorian-style gentleman's chair of the gay nineties variety. If you had been at Wittenberg any time after 1886 and well into the 1950s, you might likely recall seeing one or more of the kind of chair everyone was talking about.

Wittenberg must have had at least eighty or ninety of them, plus a number of matching two-seat settees, when the recitation hall was opened in 1886, with two new halls on the third floor for the literary societies. The *Excelsior* and *Philosophian* societies each acquired about forty-five of these chairs for their members, plus several of the two-seat settees for their anterooms where guests were received. The shiny, well-finished, and polished wood frames with shield-shaped backs, topped with beautifully carved roses, were upholstered in deep red plush-velvet seats and backs and armrests that made every member from the most senior to the bottom of the roster feel like US senators. They resembled Duncan Phyfe American Empire chairs, the kind referred to often as lolling chairs. Later when the literary societies closed for extreme lack of interest in the new student generations, the school was plagued with a huge supply of these no-longer-wanted chairs.

Over time, these chairs were dispersed to student rooms, if a student would have one. Others were relegated to the local used furniture stores or to faculty homes where they became heirlooms, and others showed up with some of the settees in various campus social-gathering lounges where they added a quaint, decorative touch. The literary societies might have disposed of them sooner if they could have afforded replacements. As a result, the school had been very lucky to find as many takers as they did.

To this day, apparently, some of these quaint relics survive, and it is one of these apparently that is haunted. The few who had become concerned about the rumor are now about the task of trying to find out more and, if possible, to identify who it was that haunted the chair. Apparently, our informant added, if you pass by rapidly or without paying the chair any attention, you will see nothing. If, on the other hand, you linger a bit and look right at it, a faint dustlike image of a fairly handsome young man becomes just barely visible. But if you are very patient and appear empathetic, very gradually, a clearer and more positive image becomes apparent. That suggests, he concluded, that the spirit haunting the chair wants to decide whom he would talk to and that he is not open to any and all comers.

Those on campus who have seen the clearer image of the man in the chair say that he wears eyeglasses, has a full, barely over-the-lip mustache, but is otherwise clean-shaven. He is well dressed in a coat and a modern four-in-hand necktie. Some have said that they believe he is a *Philosophian,* for he is of serious demeanor and very matter-of-fact. He seems about ready to debate, orate, or declaim on some urgent issue of his day. Yet before any word is heard, the image slowly fades just as it appeared. The informant reported that as it vanished, the reporter from campus heard a muffled sob, or perhaps it was only a sigh.

If there are only a half dozen or so of these Victorian gentlemen's chairs with their deep red velvet upholstery and their delicately carved roses remaining at Wittenberg, scattered about the campus, does that mean that each one has its own private ghost? Or does the same sobbing or sighing *Philosophian* occupy only one of the chairs? Or can he be found at one time or another in all the others? Someone has suggested that upon death, one's soul breaks into three parts, and therefore, one personality could be in more than one place at the same time. Could this apparition thus be in three chairs at once? That does not seem to help much in resolving our dilemma and only adds to the confusion. Perhaps the spirit of any former literary society member could visit the chairs, making them an open channel between his past world and the present one. There, you can see the full weight and extent of the variety of questions arising among those whose attention has been attracted to this mysterious situation. "Such is the excitement over the matter," the informant told me, "that there is a greatly revived interest on the part of many in acquiring one of these chairs."

By the time any report of these casual vigils at the chairs had wafted its way to the outlanders, some time had passed, and the reports had grown out of all proportion as they traveled, adulterated in a score of retellings. It seems that the collective conclusion, however, is that the ghost of the chair is one fairly handsome, youngish, bespectacled and mustached, stylishly dressed, almost dapper sobbing or sighing *Philosophian,* and him alone. There is no agreement on the ghost's identity and only speculation about why he is there or what he is trying to accomplish. He had not lingered long enough, apparently, for any such questions to be raised, let alone answered.

It will be some time yet before the informant has any reasonable speculation on any of these matters. He told the reporter from campus he was beginning to think that he might have to go to campus to make his own investigation. He had often thought of making such a visit just for sentimental reasons, but had hesitated to do so because he feared that when he got there, everything would be different from what he remembers. There would be no one there whom he would know or who remembered him, and he would feel very much out of place at the modern school. Not only do we attend school when we are very young and impressionable but also we grow into someone else after we graduate. The school changes too as new generations of students and faculty supplant us. We ourselves, though still living, become mere ghosts to the new residents in a place most different. The despairing man in the chair, he was convinced, was "a ghost-a-borning" like the rest of us and is just discovering who he is in a strangely different but once familiar place.

The informant found a room in a quaint old inn ran by Bob and Martha near the campus and planned on a good night's sleep to bolster his spirits for a day's sleuthing about some of Wittenberg's old chairs. The next morning, he would hunt down the Victorian gentleman's chair in question, coax the gentle ghost to appear, and then gently question him. He had been warned, he said, about his venture and told to be careful by old Gregory. He said some few of us are more sensitive than others to these ghosts of the past, and once they find out that you are in that category, they will give you no peace, seeking to involve you in their enterprise.

When he fell asleep that night, he dreamed he had returned to the Wittenberg of his own day and was surprised to see that everything was exactly as he remembered it. He also noted quite a number of the old literary society chairs still in use here and there. When he found the correct chair and coaxed its reticent ghost to talk to him he learned that he had been in that chair a very long while, too reticent to catch any one's attention, and growing more despondent with every passing year.

The gentle ghost had been a freshman in the 1885-86 school year, he told him, the year that Recitation Hall became ready for occupancy. He had joined the *Philosophian Society* that very fall because of their calm and generally reflective demeanor and helped move the society into its new quarters. He was among the very first to sit in the society's beautiful new Victorian gentlemen's red velvet chairs. And with that, he had begun a very positive and productive lifelong love affair with Wittenberg College. What surprised the listener most was that he knew right away who this haunted soul was—or had been—and it startled him so much that he awakened immediately and sat bolt upright in his bed, wide-eyed with a strong pulse beating through his body. He knew who the ghost was, and he suspected why he was there.

It was not that they had been in school together, far from it, for he had graduated many years before our informant. He only knew him by name. His face was familiar because he had seen his photograph in old Wittenberg yearbooks, the kind that are no longer produced. In his day at Wittenberg, the ghost's name was still very well known because he had had so much to do with designing the Wittenberg that still existed many years later. Students still heard his name almost daily. Before he realized that he knew who our ghost was, he had said that he probably would not tell anyone who he was if he knew. Now he questioned whether it was fair to this ghost of the chair to keep silent.

As a student, our ghost had organized the school's first male glee club with the expressed purpose of serenading the ladies who were becoming more numerous in the new coeducational Wittenberg. So great was his rapport with his fellow students that it was he who had proposed that the school's colors should be cardinal and cream as the school's athletic spirit rapidly increased. Also, it was he who had composed Wittenberg's first cheer for the statewide literary society contest among the state's many colleges and then applied it to meet the needs of the athletic teams thereafter.

> Rah, Rah, Rah,
> Rah, Rah, Rah,
> Rah, Rah, Wittenberg
> Bing, Boom, Bah—h—h.

While a graduate student at Columbia University in New York City, Robert H. Hiller's Phi Kappa Psi brothers at Wittenberg sent him lyrics, now forgotten and it's just as well, for a song they wanted to sing at a chapter party to entertain their guests. They asked him to compose a lively tune, and he did so. It has survived to this day. He reported that its catchy rhythm was that of New York City's elevated train as the speeding car's wheels clacked across the rail connections as he rode from the university to a Fifth Avenue church where he was the organist and choir director.

In 1913, he reused that same tune for a new Alma Mater hymn for Wittenberg. Thereafter, students sang at the lively clickety-clack pace of the elevated until alma mater singing became more solemn and more dignified. He had returned to Wittenberg as professor of Greek, a subject of declining popularity, and of Art and Music that saw growing student interest. Later in his life, he made a gift to Wittenberg to remodel the chapel in Recitation Hall. In gratitude, the school named it Hiller Chapel. It was the school's chapel for seventy years, from 1886 until 1956, when President Stoughton built Weaver Chapel. Former US president Theodore Roosevelt was probably Hiller Chapel's most famous speaker in all those years. The students had greeted him with a single boisterous cheer of "Teddy Rah," and the crowd filled the chapel until there was standing room only, and the crowd flowed out its doors and up and down the two stairways and out on to the campus walks.

Our informant wondered what could have brought Robert H. Hiller, class of 1889, from the great Wittenberg life he had led to his present state of despair. He might have whispered,

> Just think about it, my literary society is gone, barely remembered. Only these old chairs remain of all that it was. No one remembers the glee club since it merged with the women's glee club to form the Wittenberg Choir. Even the school's official colors have bleached from Cardinal and Cream to Red and White. No longer do you hear a rousing 'Rah, Rah, Rah' from well-drilled crowds. Cheer leading is no longer the dynamo driving an explosive student spirit. It in itself has become almost a spectator sport, something of a side show. Seldom does anyone sing Wittenberg's Alma Mater and never at the pace of the New York elevated. A recent president even joked about it with new students telling them they only had to sing it twice in four years; at the opening assembly for new students and at commencement. Otherwise, singing it was voluntary. Do seniors any longer choke-up as they sing the final verse?

> > Wittenberg, dear Wittenberg,
> > Time flies fast away,
> > Soon our happy college days,
> > Will be gone for aye,

But in all life's storm and stress,
What ere we may do,
To our Alma Mater dear
We will ere be true.

Please, faster; and with a little more syncopation!

As the ghost in the chair sang that last verse of his alma mater, he did not rise and stand as students had always done. He was too weak. As he sang, his image in the red velvet chair that had grown quite bright as we talked began to fade, and as he finished, his image vanished altogether. He was insistent that he heard not a sob but a great sigh from this polite and gallant ghost as he faded from his view.

WILLIAM A. KINNISON

CHAPTER 18

A Ghostly Wedding

THE STORY I now relate was one that I cannot vouch for because I was not there. Nor do I believe it really happened. Yet there were those who belatedly assured the public that it occurred and was one of the most exciting developments in the world of spiritualism in the late nineteenth century.

It was a story told to me by someone who heard it told at a class fiftieth reunion many decades ago. It allegedly brought, she said, the "here" and the "hereafter" together, just outside Hiller Chapel at Wittenberg. Those who were certain of its having happened were very upset by their inability to convince others that it, in fact, took place as they described. Only the few, it seemed to her, who escaped reality for a time, remained persistent in their assertions. She said that weddings, however, except for the most socially emaciated among us, were always events most happily regarded, full of hope and love and joy. It is in that spirit that I am willing to tell this tale at all.

So quietly and discreetly was the event handled that not even the local newspapers caught wind of it and thus failed to reveal it to the outside world when it occurred. Similar events scattered about the country were mentioned in other papers from time to time but were generally ignored by more sober and reasonable people. The event at Wittenberg was remarkable in that as many mortals as were said to be involved, none seemed to have talked of it until long after the event was said to have happened.

The story was related by an alumna many years afterward. It is at such events, especially fiftieth reunions, that a president hears such confessions, by then safely shrouded in the mists of misremembered time. At the time of this alleged event, the confessor, a woman, could have been a sophomore. The more she tried to convince the then president that she had observed the event, the more he suspected that she must have been something more than just another face in the crowd.

As it was told to me, it was after midnight on a night with a full moon, a so-called blue moon. The campus literally glowed in the moonlight. It was so bright that every building, tree, and walking path was clearly visible. The informant said she thought she saw a crowd of people—some more distinct than others—gathering at Recitation Hall. She decided, she said hesitantly, to join them. She had not heard by the grapevine of any great sortie planned for that night by any class or any other bit of mischief by one group or another. But she was not going to miss out. She sounded unconvincing, my informant said, in her own explanation of how she got involved.

Every college, in addition to printed rules, had some unwritten basic assumptions that were considered to be foundational. One of those at Wittenberg and virtually all other collegiate institutions of the day was that no student could be married while enrolled. If you married, you withdrew from school. By the early nineteenth century, students had begun to challenge such a rule. Some at nearby Miami University in Oxford, Ohio claimed it would improve student behavior, relax tensions, and improve morality. They did not prevail.

Somewhere along the way, well into the twentieth century, it was said a daughter of the then sitting president of Wittenberg ran off to Indiana and married her true love—another student—about whom she was more excited than her parents. Under the circumstances, this foundational principle that students could not be married was rendered at that moment archaic and abandoned.

The wedding we are concerned about occurred some fifty years before the rule was dropped. If word had gotten out about this event, it was doubtful that much discussion would have resulted. The idea of student ghosts marrying would not have been taken very seriously at all. It would have been dismissed as a particularly antireligious stunt.

The ghost wedding was brought about, apparently, by an amateur student medium on campus in a séance, or sitting, in the wide hallway just outside the north entrance to Hiller Chapel on the second floor of the

WILLIAM A. KINNISON

recitation hall. Séances, apparently, had become popular entertainment for some of the more demonstrative students as spiritualism became more popular in the society at large. A séance was a gathering of six to ten amicable people under the auspices of a practicing spiritualist or medium who claimed that they could contact the world of the dead and bring a departed soul back to communicate with one or more of those present. One can only speculate on how many audacious students of the 1870s and 1880s could be found who would undertake such proceedings and particularly one involving such a large gathering of humans and of the departed as would attend this mysterious wedding.

Well, obviously, several individuals at Wittenberg assumed they had such skills and practiced such rites on any number of dull and quiet campus evenings on the front porch of some home or in an offered parlor, perhaps even the social parlor of Ferncliff Hall, the residence of the women students. It was all good fun and could be attempted without the need of crystal balls or Ouija boards—common instruments, I was told—for reaching the beyond. In the séance, simply by holding hands in a darkened room, students could see what they might be able to make happen. Only undergraduates would think they could bring a whole host of spirits together with a large gathering of mortals and have them dance and sing together as if they were all in the same club.

Two sisters, it seemed, had roomed together in Ferncliff Hall but had had less than satisfactory experiences in their private lives and had left the campus for home. Their parents were insisting that the two must marry men that they approved of and that the older must marry before the younger. The younger had died of a broken heart because her parents had absolutely forbidden her to marry the man she loved. She had met him at Wittenberg, but her parents insisted he was not of their social level and just "too different" to fit in with their community and class. The other had dutifully submitted and had done what was expected and married the man chosen for her. She was, to all appearances, happy in that choice. Ferncliff Hall residents who had known the two sisters wanted to contact the remaining one to express their condolences. As they whiled away a particularly uneventful evening in the Ferncliff lounge, the thought occurred to them that they might also try to contact the deceased sister through a séance.

The Flying Dutchman, whose story I related first, was said never to have visited Ferncliff Hall because none of its rooms had a very long history for him to relate. David Burger, on the other hand, had willingly extended his duties as the host of Wittenberg Hall to include the ladies' hall as well. He saw himself as their host, guardian, and protector. Many residents over the few years of its existence, it seemed, had met him. They decided to hold a séance with the expressed purpose of contacting Davey and asking his help in locating their former dorm mate who had passed away.

Not because of the uncertain skills of the student medium but because of Davey's eagerness to help, the group made almost immediate contact with him. And he was quite receptive of the task of finding the spirit of the young lady they sought. He had appeared at the very first calling of the medium; indeed he was already in the room, we are told, watching unseen from behind the heavy window drapes in the hall parlor. They should have noticed how cool the room was when they entered. It became even cooler when he brought the young lady's spirit into the room with them. She seemed tense yet purposeful and spoke immediately without waiting for questions or hearing what those who called for her wanted to say.

She wanted to immediately marry her beloved and asked her former friends to help her. She wanted a ceremony on campus, in Hiller Chapel if possible, and wanted Pastor Joel Schwartz to perform the ceremony. He was, she stopped to add, the first ever to bear the title of campus pastor at Wittenberg in 1866. She hurried on. She wanted a short reception following the ceremony in the beautiful formal garden behind the recitation hall. It was, she noted, the most beautiful spot on the beautiful campus. From all I have heard, she was correct in that description. The garden had existed from the school's earliest days until the middle of the twentieth century when it gave way to the Reci annex and a staff parking lot.

The séance ended almost immediately after she finished speaking. Davey indicated that he would see to all the arrangements for the spirit world if the students attending would contact the living. The conversation ended, the room warmed immediately, and the excited students talked loudly and rapidly about what they had just experienced, wondering if it had really happened or was some strange-kind of self-hypnosis to which they had all succumbed.

Some weeks later, my informant said, the mortals and the spirits gathered once more just outside Hiller Chapel. The teller of the tale did not explain how they were summoned this time or by whom. Presumably it was another séance held quietly in the hallway. It was just after that event that my informant had begun her story. "As I came closer to Reci by a circuitous route from Ferncliff Hall across Kissing Bridge and up the small incline to Reci to the formal garden behind the building, I noticed a white floral arch in the bright moonlight. It was a wedding arch, I was certain." She continued, telling him that some who were gathering did not know who the bride was but knew the groom; others knew the groom but not the bride. Most, if not all, had not received a formal invitation. Neither set of parents was there. Everyone knew somehow not to bring gifts or extra guests. Pastor Schwartz was clad in the austere Puritan black in the custom of the Americanized Lutherans

The bride wore a tiara in her hair and was dressed in white in a modest dress and completely enveloped in a long white veil. She was attended by two bridesmaids; one of whom was her living sister, but the other was unknown to those who saw her. When they appeared, the bride asked those near them, "Do we not look like the three graces—elegance, beauty, and the love of life?"

The groom appeared almost as if dressed in white light. He wore knee breeches, stockings, and buckled shoes. He was more smartly dressed than anyone present who knew him had ever seen. Shortly, his image was even more distinct: a face of strong features, with keen black eyes and an overhanging square forehead. His prominent nose was less obtrusive now and his face fuller and more rounded. To the great delight of all, the groom, quite clearly of a class not acceptable to the bride's parents, someone she had met one dark and lonely night in Ferncliff

Hall, was the genial and gentlemanly ghost and host of Wittenberg Hall himself—David Burger.

Those present were almost evenly divided between mortals and spirits, and they were seated alternatively at the ceremony but mingled freely at the reception. Never had such diversity existed at Wittenberg. Various delicacies and beverages were served. The spiritus frumenti, far exceeded the school rules about what beverages were allowed to be served at campus events, but that seemed irrelevant to those gathered together. As the reception progressed, at about three o'clock in the morning, the ghosts in attendance began to fade, and all departed hurriedly, including Mr. and Mrs. David Burger. Nothing had been said to anyone about the wedding trip.

Only the living remained conversing among themselves. The temperature gradually rose in the garden, an occurrence they all commented on as they departed. One might have expected that our red-headed doom-saying friend the Flying Dutchman with his smelly pipe would have been present for the ghostly lovers' wedding, but he did not seem to be present based on the story as told to me. Also, the first bridesmaid was the bride's living sister, and I always suspected thereafter that the second bridesmaid was the very woman who had first told the story of the ghostly wedding many, many years ago.

CHAPTER 19

The Wittenberg Inn

IMAGINATION CAN BE a great spawning ground for ghosts—seemingly real people in possibly real but more likely fictional places that somehow erratically occupy our brains. "What might have been" just like "What used to be" and "what we wished had happened" and "What will be" are alive in our minds and can jumble our memories of what happened, creating ghostlike images that seem to be real.

Such is the wonderful world of the Wittenberg Inn on Jefferson Square, just two handsome blocks from the Tiger Stadium and Wittenberg's modern overshadowing new athletic complex. The complex is perhaps far more satisfying to the modern eye than Wittenberg's extremely modest "old gym" of the 1890s. That old gray (actually white-washed) wood-frame structure that briefly hovered north of the recitation hall and west of Wittenberg Hall, before being moved in parts to the athletic fields north of the campus, was smaller than a basketball court. That sport had not yet emerged in student interest but did soon after the turn of the century. Yet it was in that peripatetic old gym—for yes, it moved around the campus—that Wittenberg's great athletic spirit was born. From it, a thousand ghosts emerge. The old gym started where Koch Hall is now located, was moved bodily to the athletic fields north of campus, and when torn down its entrance hall, was retained as a ticket booth for the playing field. Some of its boards are reported to have been used in the building of the Wittenberg Inn.

Finally, as plans developed for a new field house built of brick, the old gym was scheduled to be torn down. On Halloween in October 1929, the Wittenberg Women's Athletic Association gave a farewell party in the building, symbolically burying the old gym. It was a gala campus-wide party, born out of student enthusiasm for the new building. Students wore fantastic, even outrageous, costumes and every sort of mask reflective of ghosts, skeletons, and creatures from beyond the grave. Pretend gypsies told fortunes, and other seers foretold a future that never came. There was a pumpkin relay race, with the strongest of the men carrying the largest and heaviest pumpkins they could handle while running the hundred-yard dash. Everyone danced all around the old gymnasium amid corn shocks, pumpkins, and orange-and-black crepe paper. Bounteous refreshments were served, and every one said afterward that it was the greatest party of the year.

The inn too was small and cozy, like the old gym, though an imagined place, well managed by our genial hosts Bob and Martha. It was the infrequent gathering place for many of our really "old boys" to use that quaint English term for alumni, and nowadays we add "old girls" as well. Bob always said jokingly that when he retired from the Wittenberg history department, he and Martha would run a bed-and-breakfast or something like that. She would sing when appropriate, in solo, or in a quartette of friends and oversee the cooking and housekeeping. Bob would sit, rocking on the porch, entertaining the guests with stories of the American Civil War or miscellaneous campus reminiscences.

In retirement, he looked more and more like Robert E. Lee, with his graying hair and beard taking on the shape of Lee's and the shade of confederate gray. Bob, as we all know, was never a captive of the lost cause and never gave credence to its political and economic value system. He was no Civil War rebel monument waiting to be torn down in a new day. He often recounted for guests the weekend that the Tigers played at Gettysburg College, and Bob went along to give the squad a lecture tour of the battlefield where the tide in that war began to turn in the favor of the North and against the confederacy. Like the old innkeeper in Longfellow's *Tales of a Wayside Inn* who repeatedly told his guests the story of the "Midnight Ride of Paul Revere," Bob would tell inn guests what he told the Tigers that day—the Battle of Gettysburg.

The tavern at the inn is the most popular place on Friday nights before the big game at Wittenberg on Saturday afternoons. Ideally, it is always a cold, crisp, and sunny day, but not too cold and crisp. No one remembers the days of cold drenching rains, but they remember

Earl, chairman of the Board of Directors and his wife, Jean in their well-seasoned ponchos. The forecast is always for a beautiful, perfect game day. That makes for a perfect Friday night with the tavern's huge fireplace roaring as the array of interesting and unusual guests gather and the room fills with a stout array of truly loyal and believing fans. They confidently make plans for the inevitable postgame victory party the next day.

The tavern walls, as you can imagine, are covered with sports pictures, memorabilia, and trophies from the earliest times to the present. Each one triggers a host of stories from the genial crowd. The warmth and friendly banter is often sidetracked as obvious differences appear. One person's remembered tale contradicts another's, but such incidents are always rapidly and cordially resolved by combining both views in a newer and ever-growing tale. Soon the room seems to be full of ghosts of players from other days, recreating their former glories right there in the middle of the room. All the guests are standing, energetically waving their arms and cheering loudly, reaching out as if to touch the heroes dancing before them. Robert Hiller rises from his red velvet chair to better organize the cheers. Who would be courageous enough to even whisper that this was not real? Yesterday's sports heroes are alive again, almost within touch, having one more great moment before giving way to the next story. You can see it live or in instant replay.

It is remarkable that you can sit in an empty stadium or a deserted gymnasium, even in the tavern of the Wittenberg Inn, and hear the roar of crowds cheering yesterday's heroes. They look up to you, smiling broadly and waving with the joy of victory and the sense of a job well done. There is no greater crowd of witnesses to the possibility of human immortality than the now gone athletes and vanished fans of the long ago Greek games. The closest any man could come to the immortal gods was to have won an athletic contest at Olympia. Towns were renamed with your name. Mothers named their sons after you. Even our school's famed motto "Having Light We Pass It on to Others" is derived from Plato's description for Socrates of a competitive relay race on horseback, with fiery torches as the batons, in a race held annually in honor of the goddess Athena. Actually, the response in our motto is an excited question: "Will they carry torches and pass them to one another?" Students who knew Greek better than they do today correctly translated it when they named the student newspaper the *Torch*.

A certain ghost to be recalled sooner or later any Friday night at the tavern is the handsome and energetic Curtis Laughbaum who played football for Wittenberg through four years of college, then three more years while he was in the seminary, and then once more when he returned for a postgraduate course. He played in 1897, 1898, 1899, 1900, 1901, 1902, 1903, and 1905. He broke his collarbone in the nineteenth century and his nose in the twentieth. No one gave his long career in the early days of intercollegiate football a second thought.

Another star who will inevitably make his appearance on a Friday night is Bob Bescher. He came to Wittenberg in 1905, having played for Notre Dame. He was described as a lusty athlete, a great give and take fellow, rugged and full of fun. In two seasons at Wittenberg, he carried the ball one thousand seven hundred yards in twelve games, scored fifteen touchdowns, and did all the punting. At six feet, 190 pounds, he was the fastest man on the field. He also played baseball and later played outfield with the Cincinnati Reds. His speed at stealing bases led Grantland Rice, a sportswriter, to call him the ghost of the bases.

Sooner or later, someone will call T. W. "Bill" Stobbs to the assemblage as one of the greatest coaches in Wittenberg history. He coached during the depression and the years leading up to World War II. He was, all at the same time in those tight-budget years, a coach of football, basketball, and baseball. He took his teams to championship level in all three sports. In football, he was a single-wing coach and, as such, had few peers in the nation. He won state championships in football in 1933 and 1940; in basketball, he had outstanding teams in 1937–1938, 1938–1939, and 1939–1940; he won the Ohio Conference baseball championship in 1937–1938 and placed second in 1938–1939.

The favorite stories for some were the games Wittenberg played against Ohio State, winning as many games as they lost. The favorite story of all time, according to John L. Zimmerman, class of 1879, was Wittenberg's great team of 1896. It was the school's fourth year of intercollegiate football and one never to be forgotten. The feature of the summer preseason was an intercollegiate football round-robin tournament at the Ohio State Fair where five of the state's leading schools participated: Akron, Denison, Miami, Ohio State, and Wittenberg.

The grand prize was eighteen spiffy new team uniforms awarded to the school with the highest cumulative score when all the games were completed. As it turned out, Wittenberg won the prize and beat Ohio State, 6–0 in the process. Thus, Wittenberg entered its fourth season with the team decked out in all new uniforms and high spirits.

"John L," as Zimmerman was affectionately known, invariably chuckled when he added another tidbit of information to this remarkable tale. The Wittenberg team, as it left Springfield for Columbus and the state fair, stopped by the Big Four Railroad yards to pick up two burly young yardmen to beef up its line for the big tournament. Such were the freewheeling days of intercollegiate sports in those early years.

One issue that always stirred up a lot of heated discussion is where the Tigers got their nickname in the first place. The varied viewpoints seemed mostly informed by a total lack of any reasonable official explanation. Like so many things in the early days, decisions were made as events, and problems evolved. Wittenberg teams were at first known in the newspapers as the Fighting Lutherans, and the school authorities thought that was quite sufficient and resisted any change. All the school's earliest coaches had all come for short stints after graduating from Princeton University where the teams were known as the Tigers.

After several such coaches in a row and years of encouragement on the field to "play it like tigers," it was quite possible that Wittenberg athletes saw themselves as the "tigers of the west," regardless of what they were called officially. The Tigers nickname was only used sporadically in the press beginning in the 1920s while the official name remained the Fighting Lutherans. To sharpen the argument in 1936, rooters for the basketball team suggested they call the team the "Wittenberg Red Devils," hoping the school could be provoked into accepting Tigers as a better choice. In the mid-1940s, two clowns Ezry and Torchy appeared in the student paper, opening a final phase of the battle over a name.

Ezry, named after Wittenberg's first president, was a white-trousered, red-letter-sweatered, long-legged tiger cartoon clown. He was the artistic creation of John Norris, '50, a World War II veteran and an art major. He introduced his tiger on March 22, 1946. Ezry was first named Atom in keeping with the times. In the fall of 1947, with the face of Atom, the body of a human collegian, and the head of a tiger, Ezry was going through rush advocating delayed pledging as a needed reform of the fraternity system. It softened up the administration by endorsing something it wanted. Yet Ezry, said Norris, was created with the serious purpose in mind as a "cartoon sports trademark" to lock in "Tigers" as the official name of Wittenberg athletic teams after years of struggle. "Torchy," an assertive coed tiger companion for a bashful Ezry, soon made her debut. With Tiger suits and papier-mâché heads, Ezry and Torchy dominated football games and all other athletic events for over a decade. Wittenberg Tigers then unequivocally became the nickname for all the school's intercollegiate teams. Soon all the fans were Tigers too.

Perhaps we should hasten to complete our story since our imaginary Wittenberg Inn will disappear promptly at 3:00 a.m. as scheduled, to reappear the following Friday. Our old friend Gregory will soon be here to close things up. The guests begin to fade, the fire dwindles, and our hosts retire.

There is one more story, however, that our guests like to recall. It is the story of the Indian skull trophy that went each year to the winner of the Wittenberg–Ohio Wesleyan football game. During the depression of the 1930s, schools made every effort to encourage fans to invest scarce funds in attending Saturday afternoon football games. One common move was to create a homecoming game and elect a homecoming queen to stir up interest. But the Indian skull game was pretty much the scheme of Wesleyan's "Fighting Bishops," speaking of team trademarks.

Perhaps it was in an old Native American hunting ground near Wesleyan that the students found the skull. In their exuberance, they just assumed it was an Indian skull and attached it to a nicely finished board. It was so important to stir up their fans for the Wittenberg game that they initiated the "battle for the skull." Wesleyan seemed to win it most in the early years and Wittenberg in the later years. In the years when the Wittenberg-Wesleyan rivalry was interrupted because the schools were in different athletic conferences, Wittenberg had the skull seemingly on permanent display because it had been the winner in the last several games the two schools played.

There among the shiny silver and brass of normal trophies glared the empty eye sockets of this rather large skull, ashen gray with black highlights, staring brazenly at every passerby. Many students saw it going to and fro in the field house every day. Perhaps most of them took little notice of it, but it always seemed to be trapped in its locked case with little possibility of ever getting out but nevertheless seemed menacing.

All that changed in the 1980s when Wittenberg and Ohio Wesleyan once again found themselves in the same conference. But times had changed, and when the two rivals were once again scheduled to fight over the skull, some faculty and students at both institutions raised the issue of the propriety of having an Indian skull trophy as the game prize. In the subsequent discussions, there appeared great uncertainty on whether it was actually an Indian skull or not. Such was the sensitivity of the use and misuse of Indian artifacts, both by Indian tribes and federal laws protecting Indian artifacts, that the two schools agreed to dispense with the game trophy. The skull was detached and given to representatives of the Shawnee tribe for an appropriate decision on the matter. The group of Tiger fans gathered at the inn could never agree whether the settlement agreed to was appropriate, always expressing a fairly wide set of differing opinions on the matter.

John L. Zimmerman on the Wittenberg board of directors and Samuel A. Ort as President were the team that opened Wittenberg to the world of intercollegiate athletics. The crowd at the tavern of the Wittenberg Inn knew and respected both men, Zimmerman more than Ort perhaps. But it was Ort who put physical fitness into the school's definition of its educational philosophy. He told the class of 1900 that the soul and the human mind and character had no other instrument through which they could express themselves in the world than the physical body. He was concerned about the growing physical weakness of professional people who often died too soon of physical maladies and frailties. He saw fitness as a crucial educational concern. The spiritual and the mental were not separate from the physical. Only with health and fitness could any human creature become what it ought to be. He told the graduating seniors, "If in the evening time of your days you can still chant your morning song, it will be because unimpaired vigor of body, strength of heart, firmness of muscle, steadiness of nerve, healthy assimilating forces of your physical organism are part of the capital with which you start to do the business of human life."

He addressed the graduates with a heavy heart because of the death of his son, just before he was to graduate in this class. He described the education they had received: "And now to have all these, a beautiful body, an improved mind, a tender conscience, a warm heart, and a Christian soul, what a solid basis for a true and honorable life!" For Ort, physical fitness through participation in sport was very humanistic. Imagine football and all sports activity as a part of the humanities.

CHAPTER 20

Take Her up Tenderly

THE SELF-ASSURED MEMORANDUM from the school's vice president to the president seemed reserved, dispassionate, professional, and a trifle apprehensive.

"A most unusual experience occurred on Tuesday, May 10, 1966," it began, "but I am pleased to report that everything is cared for even though the final details, at the time of this dictation on the morning of May 11, are not completed."

It seemed the long-forgotten story of Woodshade cemetery had crashed once more into Wittenberg's modern complacency. And one could wonder if it might not happen again.

> It was reported to me on the morning of May 10 that in the excavation work for the new science building the shovel came upon a cast iron casket. Before this was realized the lid had been broken by the shovel and the pieces had been carted off to where the land fill is taking place in Ferncliff Cemetery. Therefore, if there was any kind of a nameplate on the lid we have not yet made any attempt to find it. In the absence of the Business Manager and you, Mr. President, the workmen came to get my advice both from the legal and moral standpoints. I checked immediately with our attorney and he was as lacking in experience in such a situation as was I. I quickly checked the statutes and discovered that there was a necessity for obtaining a health permit to move a body during the months of April through September.

It was astonishing that all this was occurring one hundred and three years since Wittenberg's nineteenth-century student diarist William Settlemyer had detailed the school's careful removal of all those buried in Woodshade Cemetery to Ferncliff Cemetery in April 1863.

> This afternoon I discussed the matter over the telephone with the City Health Director and he checked with the State Board of Health. He then called back to assure me that a permit would be issued and suggested that I get in touch with an undertaker. I then went to the City Law Office and there met with the City Attorney and the City Manager. . . . We determined that the city and county had no liability in this situation because the body had been buried on private ground and it was therefore up to us. The City Manager referred us to the Director of Ferncliff who proved to be most cooperative and helpful. His staff helped with the excavation machinery that could help us complete the removal most effectively.
>
> It is known that the body is that of a woman. This burial must have taken place seventy-five to one hundred years ago. [It must have occurred some years before that if Woodshade closed in 1863.] The cast iron casket indicates affluence. Whether any identifying information will be obtained will have to await the removal which should occur on Wednesday morning and I will complete the dictation of this memorandum after that.
>
> I have just returned from witnessing the disinterment. The Ferncliff Cemetery people were most cooperative. Our Business Manager and a number of his staff were there. No kind of identification was obtainable. One of the men even shook out the glove of the left hand, but no wedding ring was found.

WILLIAM A. KINNISON

The iron casket was then loaded on a Ferncliff Cemetery truck and taken to the cemetery for reburial.

It is too bad that our records do not contain information about matters such as this but even our financial records are missing for much of the earlier years of this institution.

There is a poem appropriate for this moment by Thomas Wood entitled "The Bridge of Sighs," which Edgar Allan Poe once used as an illustration of what good poetry was.

> Take her up tenderly,
> Lift her with care,
> ....
> Touch her not scornfully,
> Think of her mournfully,
> ....

The poet then asked about her father, mother, possible sisters or brothers and whether there might have been "a dearer one" nearer to her than the others. The poet was striving to maximize the humanity of a person who, apparently, had died alone. The memo writer did not dwell on such matters and had no way of knowing such details.

Would this unknown woman be the last to be found still buried on the campus?

There was one sixty-six-year-old Springfield resident who remembers playing on the northern edge of the campus as a little boy, just off Cecil Street, now Bill Edwards Drive. His aunt lived on Pythian Avenue, and every time he stayed with her in the summer, he roamed the area. He recalled six graves at the southeast corner of Plum and Cecil Streets and four more at the foot of Pythian Avenue. That was forty-five years after all graves had been supposedly removed to Ferncliff. He recalled a name on one stone—Wanamaker—but nothing more. It seemed very unlikely that as many as ten burials could have been overlooked, but it was plausible that more than this one had been. On no other occasion since, however, has another grave been found.

Students from time to time have reported a shadow of a woman in a tan raincoat, seemingly floating down the wide stairway of the science building's great atrium. She seems lost and confused and totally unaware of the activities going on in the classrooms and laboratories. She has made no attempt to contact anyone as far as we know, nor has she caused any disturbance. This is consistent with the theory that she is the spirit of the disturbed burial reported in the above memo and has no involvement with science or mathematics or the building where she finds herself. It seems reasonable also that students and faculty in the building are very reluctant to give any credence to such stories and usually refer any who may become concerned to take the matter up with the department of psychology.

The ghost is sometimes seen in the company of two young men, lost and restless souls from Wittenberg's earliest days, from one of Wittenberg Hall's "unlucky" rooms. If they are aware of the nature of their science-building habitat, they give no evidence of it.

CHAPTER 21

The Everlasting Club

WHEN HE AWOKE, seemingly, he was in a comfortable chair in a very dark place, the darkest he could ever remember. The darkness was total with not even the slimmest of strings of light from under a door or a pinprick's worth through a shaded window, if indeed there were a door or window at all. He assumed that there must have been some way that he had gotten into this place. It was also a place that was very, very quiet—a quietness that seemed absolute, like a tomb, he imagined. Not a sound was made in the place by him as he strained to hear if any sound could come in from outside. Any sound might help him discover where he was. He could not see nor hear nor smell nor feel anything. He remembered nothing and seemed to be in that part of the mind, where as infants, we learn things before we have any language by which to remember them. The only clues are feelings and smells, dreads, inclinations or glees, or the trauma of birth itself. He imagined that he must be in one of those sensory deprivation chambers undergoing some weird test in the psychology department that some friend and classmate had talked him into participating in.

He considered that dubious possibility a sign of progress in his effort of trying to come to full consciousness and to figure out where he was. When he first became aware of being in this place, he was unable to move his arms or legs or arouse himself in any way. He was totally fatigued after having done absolutely nothing as far as he could remember. He felt paralyzed—that feeling you get when your mind awakes but your body seems to be still asleep. I think they call it sleep paralysis.

When he got so he could mentally command his body to move and it would do so, he was still very cautious. He did not try to stand or walk right away because he could not be sure of what might happen if he moved in any direction. He had no idea which direction was north by which to orient himself. He slowly extended his arms and feet while in a sitting position to see if there were any obstacles in front of him, beside him, or below or above him. He tapped the floor to see if it was firm and reliable. He stretched his legs to see how far solid footing might extend.

His body, especially his legs, was very stiff as though he had been asleep for a very long time without moving, drugged perhaps. He had not been restrained, tied to a chair, or bound hand or foot. He just felt as if, for whatever reason, he had not moved a muscle for hours. He began to search his mind, trying to recall how he might have gotten to this place. He was surprised that his mind was so murky and so slow to recapture any reality.

Where had he been? When did he come here? And why? Perhaps he was so stiff because the place had been cold, but it seemed warm enough now. As airtight as the place seemed to be, there still seemed to be enough fresh air coming from somewhere. He seemed now to become steadily more alert. Certainly he must be in a place with a very high ceiling. He looked up as if he were going to see a ceiling. He thought he heard music, perhaps even a few muted words: "Ill the wind, ill the time . . . late, late, late . . . yet we go on living . . . living and partly living . . . What is to be done?"

It was very faint. He could be mistaken; maybe he only thought he had barely heard something. He also thought for just a second that he smelled something. It was the smell of dust and staleness. His sense of smell must have been exhausted, but the slight movement of standing and looking up might have briefly refreshed it. Sooner than soon, however, both the music and the smell of dust again faded. He was aware again only of the sound of silence—a slight, virtually inaudible hissing in the depths of his ears. As he concentrated, hoping to hold on to this first real sense of where he was, he heard again the very faintest of sounds of organ music, perhaps a small orchestra, still there somewhere beyond this place where he was: "Ill wind . . . partly living . . ." It was an opening through which he tried to push his mental capacities as hard as he could to move out and away from this prison. Try as he might, it did not clear the cobwebs from his mind.

He sensed the sudden terror of a world without dimensions or structure or direction. There seemed to be nothing to measure where or what he was. There was only an emerging perception of chaos. There was no past, no sense of a present, no perception of a future. He seemed a void. Whither what or whither whom? Perhaps he was a ghost that did not know why it was there.

It took some time yet for his mind to clear, and he continued to pursue that slim thread of sound toward the reestablishment of a full recall of his trip to this dark place. It was the only alternative. The breakthrough, though he later discovered it was only partial, came as he recognized the source of those few words that he had barely made out. They were from T. S. Eliot's *Murder in the Cathedral*. That play had been performed in Weaver Chapel on the day of its dedication many years ago. They were somehow retained in some kind of time freeze and echoed anew for him on that desperate night.

Finally, it seemed clearer to him that late last night, he had been walking across a peaceful campus from old Reci to Blair Hall when, on the spur of the moment as he must have thought then, he walked up the twenty or so steps to the entrance to Weaver Chapel in the tower that connected the chapel and Thomas Memorial Library. On second thought, now he seemed certain that something had drawn his attention to this entrance, that it was not just happenstance. At this point, his mind deliberately deflected him from logic by injecting another totally irrelevant thought. It was about how unreasonable and medieval it was to have to climb so many steps to get to a chapel. It had nothing to do with the problem he was trying to solve. He then misremembered trying one of the heavy big glass doors, but it was locked as it should have been at that late hour. Without any further thought about how he had been led to this step, he tried another of those heavy doors, and lo, it was not locked, so he went in.

Once you are in the tower, on the dimly lit ceiling of that space is a chandelier of carved wood presenting an elaborate rendition of the ancient zodiac. More than a few visitors have expressed shock at such a pagan display in a Christian chapel, but the tower had been conceived of as neutral ground between faith and reason as Prexy Stoughton explained it. As you move from the tower into the chapel, there is a further anteroom full of ancient Jewish symbols, and only in the chapel itself do Christian symbols appear. It is like a sequence of chambers each with its own meaning for the alert. The library below represents the Enlightenment and the Renaissance. The neutral tower ties them together in spite of themselves.

Once you are in the tower, you can go a number of directions. You can go down the circular stair that hugs the inside wall of the tower to the library. Or you can turn left and go up some more steps into the chapel. You can go up the circular staircase into the tower, but there never has been any reason for any one of us ever to do so, he reflected. Nothing presumably ever happens further up, and no one remembers ever going up there unless it was as a member of the chapel staff. Apparently on this particular night, he must have been led there by an inner voice or some other still unremembered prod that raised the thought that he perhaps should be the brave one to go up and see what he could see up there on behalf of all his fellow students, some of whom must have wondered. Though most, he mused, gave it little thought at all. Again he recalled the words of T. S. Eliot: "Is it the knowledge of safety that draws our feet toward the cathedral?"

Whatever initial fear he might have had, apparently, was totally overcome by the excitement he felt just being where he was and able to do what he was contemplating. No one in his acquaintance, he was certain, had ever been up in that tower, and he was certain that when he could tell them about it, they would be incredulous and utterly and totally impressed. His mind, this time with sophomoric bravado, was again embroidering an explanation and motivation for his actions that kept him from discovering the real truth of his night's adventure.

Boldly, he began to ascend the stairs, he mused, while separately, he despaired that he might never regain the real knowledge of what his true adventure had been. With each step, he moved from the dimly lit entrance area up an increasingly dark stairwell. He had a small flashlight, one of those powerful new LED lights, but was afraid to use it for fear of being seen through the great glass doors of the tower entrance. As he rose higher in the darkening tower stairway, he lit it, but the light was so piercingly bright in that darkness that it actually hurt his eyes and stabbed at his brain. He immediately turned it off and had just enough time to see a sturdy door then turn the knob in darkness and go in. The absolute darkness in the room overwhelmed him, the door slammed, and he must have passed out.

When he finally awoke, in his subconscious, he began to recall incidents that at first seemed disjointed and unrelated. He listed them to see if he could piece this mystery together. Yes, we all—my little group of friends—had pondered the existence of a secret chamber in the tower. We knew of it only through rumor, but it had been frequently discussed. None of us knew anyone who had ever been in it, but the rumor was that some secret society—the Everlasting Club—gathered there sporadically. He believed that he was now in it and needed to look for evidence of the society's having been there if only he could get his wits about him. Strangely, at that point, he recalled that his mind was again distracted by a seemingly random incident from the past that was entirely irrelevant.

He recalled a vast murder of crows that had infested the entire campus circle some months ago and flown around the chapel-library tower. It was a flock so thick that it darkened the entire circle as if it were covered by a low thunder cloud. It was darker that day than we would wish even for Halloween. Anyone who crossed the campus that day never forgot it. It was, by chance, the same day they had removed Hilda Stoughton's famous pale blue parrot wallpaper from Philadelphia that had graced the huge center entry hall and circular staircase of the Prince-Davis House for forty years. Whatever else anyone might have thought about it, it was time for it to go. Those pale blue parrots, it was said later, joined the crows and flew indignantly around the tower until the day ended. It was the day, others said, that every ghost at Wittenberg—four score or more—had joined the procession and raced above us, circling with the incessant cawing and crowing of the birds.

The all but forgotten tower room had been originally envisioned as a meeting room for the school's honor societies and was to celebrate its top scholars and leaders among the students. At least that was what was promised in the campaign to raise the funds to complete the tower. For whatever reason, however, the room was not completed as planned. Perhaps it was not large enough; perhaps it was too "out of the way" and inconvenient to access. Perhaps societies such as those were to be less and less important as the times and the school and the students also changed.

All of a sudden, a bright light finally appeared in the very depths of our informant's addled brain, and he believed he was able to finally recall what had really happened to him. He said on the pathway from the Recitation Hall to Blair that night, he was passed by a group of people—he thought they were people—hurrying toward the Weaver-Thomas Tower. A while after they had entered, a great host of ghostly birds seemed to come out of the top of the tower. They appeared to be following a "great flying bird of a ghost ship" on the deck of which stood a host of the members of the *Excelsior Society* and their close friends, including many ladies from outside their rostered group.

All this happened so suddenly that even yet he could not register the specific sequence of actual events. They were still muddled. The society had always been the birthplace of action. They had invented a word to describe the behavioral goal that they exalted—"Excelsiorism." Every member was expected to be an "excelsiorist" to get something done; their name meant "ever upward." They shouted *perge modo*, meaning "go forward," and *altus et altior,* "higher and highest."

They softly chanted over and over *Perge Modo,* as a leader read aloud what they had always called the prophecy.

> If it is right to conceive of a time when Wittenberg's faculty and authorities would forget the origins and destiny of the institution and let it fail, there are those gone out from the Excelsior Society who would gather at the grave of the sainted Dr. Keller and, catching the echoes of the hymn which rose when its foundations were laid, would establish Wittenberg anew.

The group had lost a great deal of time, looking for the three-times-moved grave of Keller where they were to gather. Finally discovering it in Ferncliff Cemetery, they were rushing as if late from there to the tower. They just swept him into their group, and he had, it now appeared, swirled violently about the campus with them as they assessed the state of things. As they prepared to return to their tower room for discussion, they discovered him among them and knew he did not belong there. They then deliberately befuddled his mind, and he was still not fully recovered. They left him unconscious in the chair in that very dark room in the tower of the chapel-library where he later awoke in total confusion.

He tells me that he does not think he will ever fully recover from this experience. He was yet confused greatly about that night and had not recalled anything further that might have been said in the subsequent meeting that he thought they must have had. Sometimes his mind would have him believe that he never awoke but was still only dreaming a dream that would never end. Yet on other occasions, there were scarce moments when he was almost certain that these *Excelsiorists* left convinced that they had indeed set actions in motion that would restore everything as it should be.

I had been, as you know, a somewhat hesitant reteller of these stories about Wittenberg ghosts. I was certain in light of this story about the Everlasting Club that I would be urged to more actively and aggressively pursue the matter. Some would have me pursue the answers to this last riddle by further consulting with our friend Gregory; others urged a séance to contact Mr. and Mrs. Burger or perhaps that young man Hiller in the red velvet chair or others. For the moment, I would rest, however, with our informant's conclusion that the Everlasting Club had indeed set actions in motion.

Cover Art

Wittenberg's first building known as Wittenberg Hall, or simply Wittenberg, was constructed from 1848 to 1851. This oil painting was done by the student A. Lineaweaver between 1870 and 1874, depicting the hall and the class of 1874's memorial rock in front of the building. The rock disappeared mysteriously sometime after 1995.